Behind Closed Eyes

A Book on Meditation in the Form of a Novel

Jason Siff

VAJRA
BOOKS

Quality Fiction

double dorje

imprint

Published and Distributed 2017 by

Vajra Books

Jyatha, Thamel, P.O. Box 21779, Kathmandu, Nepal
Tel.: 977-1-4220562, Fax: 977-1-4246536
e-mail: bidur_la@mos.com.np
www.vajrabooks.com.np

cover portrait art: David Douglas

ISBN 978-9937-623-80-3

Printed in Nepal

Introduction

Behind Closed Eyes is a book on meditation in the form of a novel. I wrote it in 1999, shortly after the first draft of my book, *Unlearning Meditation*. My initial intention in writing this novel was to go inside the minds of meditators and show their struggles with certain traditional *Vipassana* meditation practices and what a process of "unlearning meditation" might look like. At that time, it seemed like the only way I could distinguish my approach to meditation, which later became called, "Recollective Awareness Meditation," was to contrast it with other *Vipassana* methods.

I have wanted to publish this book for many years, but only recently have I been motivated to do so. After 18 years, I still agree with most of what the meditation teacher says in his instructions and talks, though I would ask different questions and have longer dialogs with students if I wrote a similar book today. One thing about this novel, which I could never have predicted, is that certain strands of *Vipassana* meditation practice have moved more in the direction of Recollective Awareness Meditation over the past decade. If I had published it 18 years ago, it would have been seen as something radical, and probably would've been met with greater resistance, but now it can speak to a larger circle of *Vipassana* meditators, even though it is still outside of the mainstream.

I wrote this novel using 3 distinct voices. The first voice you will encounter is the *Knower of the Field*. He is the higher self, the witnessing consciousness, the pure knowing mind. When I was writing this novel, I felt that since most Eastern meditation teachings refer to a transcendent higher self, that character should be in this story. Even though Theravada Buddhists don't believe in a higher self, there are *Vipassana* teachers who reference a higher knowing or witnessing consciousness in their teachings. Whether there is a higher self is an interesting question to explore in meditation, and it is for that reason I see it as important to have this character in this novel.

The second type of voice is narration. The narrator in this case is the traditional third-person narrator who knows everything, and yet tries to remain a neutral reporter of events. The third type of voice belongs to each of the characters' inner experience of meditation, and is a type of stream of consciousness. These sections are informed by interviews with students and their meditation journals (though no student's journal is quoted or plagiarized), as well as descriptions of my own experiences in meditation, and fit with how people might write about their meditation sittings in detail.

I am grateful to the meditation students from the 1980s and 1990s who spoke to me openly and honestly about what was happening in their meditation sittings. This book is dedicated to Gordon Smith, who helped me start the Skillful Meditation Project in 1996, and hosted monthly sitting groups at his home in Mt. Washington, California, from 1992 to his death in 2006.

From 1994 through 2002, I was mostly teaching to small groups in Southern and Central California, with an occasional retreat in Spokane, Washington. It was a period of financial struggle and uncertainty on the outside, but it was also the second novel-writing period of my life, the first being in my twenties, when I wrote two novels (both unpublished). *Behind Closed Eyes* was written after *King Bimbisara's Chronicler* (published in 2000 by Sarvodaya Vishwa Lekha) but before *Seeking Nibbana in Sri Lanka* (published in 2008 by Vajra Books). There are 2 other novels yet to be published, written after this one, both of them historical novels that are sequels to *King Bimbisara's Chronicler*, titled *After the Parinibbana* and *The Myth of Maitreya*. Vajra Books, under the double-dorje imprint, has also accepted these books for publication.

My greatest hope in publishing this book is that it will bring the experiences of meditators into perspective for you, the reader, and also inspire you to become interested in trying out this form of meditation for yourself, if you haven't already. For those who have been practicing Recollective Awareness Meditation, may this book serve as a reference for your practice, alongside *Unlearning Meditation* and *Thoughts Are Not the Enemy* (both published by Shambhala Publications).

Jason Siff
Kathmandu, February 2017

Knower of the Field

"And the Knower of the Field, when without a body,
must be either knowing or unknowing.
If it is knowing, there is something for it to know,
and if there is something for it to know,
it is not liberated."

Acts of the Buddha, Canto XII.80
Ashwaghosa (circa 2nd Century A.D.)
translated by E. H. Johnston

I am the Knower of the Field. I am not human, nor am I a god nor demon. Those designations do not touch me. I exist between the ultimately real and the imaginary. Some may claim that I reside in the heart, knowing all of its secrets. Others may see me as the mind's awareness of all things within the field of consciousness. I am that and greater than that. I can see beyond the horizon of consciousness and thus know what seems impossible for anyone to know. I can tunnel beneath the secrets of the heart to where the unknown core of one's being lies. Nothing within one escapes my knowing. Yet I cannot know myself, for I am empty, devoid of my own content. I have no world but that of the mind I know. Each individual has but one Knower of the Field, and no two of us are exactly alike.

Narration

Penelope is 27 years old, a towering sleek woman, with wavy thick black hair down past her shoulders. She looks strikingly

Native American, being one-quarter, with her high cheekbones, oval eyes and jagged nose, though her skin is drained of color, white like the moon. Her brown eyes are sad, moist, often betraying her heart's true emotion as her face remains firm.

Kevin is 31 years old, a small thin man who is prematurely going bald and gray at the same time. His face is soft and smooth, with a longish nose and smallish mouth. His eyes are mostly empty of feeling, an undisturbed aqua blue, while his emotions are predominantly expressed in nose twitches and lip curls.

Penelope is a probation officer and Kevin is her supervisor. She had a conversation with him one day, over coffee, at her desk, piled high with manila folders containing the files of her charges. She assumed that he wanted to ask her about a new case, a 13-year-old gang banger who killed a convenience store clerk when he was 11 and is now out of juvenile hall and back in his parents' custody. But she was wrong. It was not about work. Kevin wanted to talk to her about his life. He was "burned out." As he said it, he sighed with shame and made a movement to get up from his chair and walk away. She said she understood, but she didn't really. Kevin believed she understood and so stayed and asked her what he could do about it, since he could not leave his job. He had a family to take care of. That cleared the air for her, as she was unsure whether Kevin's burn-out was in fact an attempt to kindle a flame. She felt she could open up a little, tell him what had helped her when she was physically exhausted and emotionally depleted from work. There was always someone, her charges usually, her superiors sometimes, sabotaging her efforts to help change the lives of kids whose lives really can't change that much. She did not see that she was not suited for the job she had. Whereas Kevin was. He did great work with the youths and was adept at dealing with his superiors and the department regulations. Since he was so proficient, and always desired to be of service, he took on more and more work, enough for 2 people in his position, and that, over time, has led to him being legitimately burned out.

Anyhow, Penelope had one bit of advice to give. She suggested to Kevin that he learn how to meditate. She has been meditating for 3 years and reminded him that just last year she asked him for time off to go on a week-long retreat. He asked her what kind of meditation it was, did he have to say "Om" or anything like that. No, he didn't. It was *Vipassana Meditation*. Most people called it, *"Insight Meditation."* Kevin seemed genuinely interested, so she went on to tell him that it did not involve rituals, prayers, mantras, or even a belief in Buddhism. All one had to do was sit still and be in the present moment. He smiled, and made a joke about how hard could it be to be in the present moment. Then he got up and went back to work. A few days later, at the end of the work day, he called Penelope into his office and asked her how he could find out about *Vipassana Meditation* retreats. He had given it a lot of thought and would like to try it. She gave him the name of a periodical that listed all the local retreats. That was the last time they talked about it.

Now Kevin is on a 10-day meditation retreat, taking off a week plus 2 days, 7 work days altogether. Penelope feels somewhat envious, though her predominant feeling is pride at being the one who gave Kevin the idea. He has told everyone at work that he was going on a family vacation, but he let her know the truth. She likes keeping people's confidences. She also imagines some kind of new bond forming between Kevin and her, a spiritual connection, and that they could go to the same sitting group together. Her boyfriend, Erik, who introduced her to *Vipassana*, will be pleased as well. Perhaps they will meet after Kevin's retreat.

Penelope daydreams about forming her own sitting group now that she and Erik have put their respective households together in preparation for a solid commitment sometime in the future. Erik's feelings are complex and Penelope prefers color-coding them to looking closely at them. She knows she loves him and imagines he loves her and refuses to go any further with her thinking. One thing meditation has taught her has been to reel her mind back in once it has gone off into some unprofitable direction.

Back at her desk, with the stack of manila folders in front of her, she puts her mind on her job. Each folder is a young life gone wrong. She can't get that thought out of her head whenever she skims the contents. These kids have done some really bad things, inconceivable things, things she would rather not know about. And yet here it is in black and white. One 12-year-old attacked a teacher, another set fire to a mini-mall, another beat up a classmate and stole his tennis shoes, and the list of crimes and offenders goes on and on, an endless river of hatred, greed, and delusion. Her own levels of these 3 poisons are so much less than what she sees in these kids that she could mistakenly see herself as pure, upright, and without blame. She just can't see her own poisons all that clearly. Her meditation practice has not gone that far yet. She is still trying to stay with the breath.

Kevin's Meditation

I sit down cross-legged on the meditation mat on the floor. Everyone in the meditation hall is doing the same. Some bow to the Buddha statue in the front, others just clasp their hands over their chest in salutation. I just sit down on the cushion and cross my legs. This is my first meditation retreat. I am looking to change my life; that is all. If I get enlightened, that is fine too. Right now I am anxious. I want the teacher to start giving instructions. I want to close my eyes and dive right in, like I see some of the others doing. They know what the instructions are. I don't. Please hurry up and give me instructions! This waiting is interminable. What if I just close my eyes and begin? And then what? I can't meditate without instructions. I will be doing it wrong.

Wait for the teacher to speak, I tell myself, repeating it over and over like a mantra, but I know I repeat it out of nervousness and for no other reason. Then he speaks. I am sitting so far back I can't see him. What is he saying? I can't understand his accent. Where does he come from? India? Wherever he comes from, his English is difficult to understand, even if I could hear his voice clearly.

Then all the people whose eyes were closed open them. I see their hands go up to their chests, palms touching, fingers pointed skywards. I do the same. The hall is filled with people saying some sort of prayer in unison. I try to imitate and keep up with them, but it is not possible. I stop trying and take a deep breath, putting my attention on listening. I close my eyes and seem to hear better. When they end, I hear the teacher say something in English about not killing, not stealing, not having sexual contact, not lying, not taking intoxicants, not eating after noon, not watching dances or plays and not listening to music, not wearing jewelry and not using scented products.

This sounds like good set of rules to meditate by.

Finally, he says something about meditation instructions. But it is still hard for me to make out every word he says. Fortunately, he repeats himself often.

He says, "Watch your breath," which I take as the instruction, and then I make out, "at the nostrils." Another instruction. I can do that. Now I can close my eyes and meditate. But the teacher goes on talking. He says things about the breath being natural and not forced... thoughts will arise to lead our minds astray... ignore them completely... do not move when feeling pain... all things are impermanent!

That is certainly enough instruction. Now be quiet and let me meditate!

But no, he has to add a few well-chosen words on what a great opportunity this is, how much it will benefit ourselves and all beings, and that we should all determine to make an end to desire and the suffering that comes from it. I agree, I agree, I agree. Now let's be quiet and meditate!

And that's it. The hall is filled with silence, which is soon replaced by the sounds of people sniffling, coughing, breathing. It is all so irritating. Each moment, at least one person out of the hundred or so people meditating here makes a sound. And I am forced to hear it. How will I ever be able to focus solely on the breath?

It is like this at home, only worse. There is always someone talking, or watching TV, doing laundry, banging about in the kitchen, flushing the toilet or taking a shower. Then the sounds of the neighbors, the street outside, and the airplanes above. I try to block out this noise when I sit alone in silence. I thought meditation would help me not be bothered by noise. It is having the opposite effect.

Must bring my attention to my nostrils. Can I feel the breath touch my upper lip on the way out? Nope. Can I feel the breath going into my nose? Yep. There it is. It is a tight, unpleasant feeling inside my nose. As I notice it, it begins to hurt. Perhaps I am breathing too hard. I need to slow down my breathing. Relax. It does not slow down. I am anxious. What if my breathing will always be heavy, fast, painful? I can't sit here for an hour like this. What am I doing here?

My wife kissed me good-bye, wishing me well, telling me what a great adventure this would be, and she would like to hear all about it. She had to stay home with the kids. My 2 daughters, who are 10 and 12. That's pretty old considering I just turned 31 last month. I was a young dad. I began working for the Probation Department after my second born. I wanted to be a psychologist, but I needed to make a secure living, and with a Bachelor's in Psychology, I could easily work for Probation. Besides, I wanted to get started on a career when I had a family to support.

After I turned 27, I went back to school to become a psychotherapist. I had enough first-hand experience with troubled youths to know that I could do therapeutic work with people. I enrolled in a night class and soon got an internship at a counseling center that mostly treated couples in crisis. The experience was eye-opening. An average couple would come in with the problem of feeling distant and disconnected, and by the third or fourth week, it would come out that one of them was having an affair, or had been contemplating divorce, or had spent all of the combined savings, or some such marital disaster. I kept seeing this pattern over and over again. It made me wonder about my own marriage. What if we got down to the heavy stuff in our relationship? Would we survive as a couple?

I began to feel depressed and no longer wanted to see clients. I dropped out of school, telling my wife that I was not cut out to be a therapist. She disagreed, and we argued about that for the next year. She was hoping that I could have a well-paying job where I could make my own hours and then share more equally in raising our 2 girls. No way was I going to try to get at what was beneath that. I would rather we argued over trivial matters and disappointed each other in predictable ways than deal the death blow to our marriage. Still, things were not that good between us. We both needed more time apart. Which is how I got her to agree to allow me to go on this 10-day meditation retreat. In her mind, I guess, I am supposed to come out of this a changed man, one who is friendly, generous, loving, and capable of living in harmony with her. Not if it continues to go like this.

Ouch! A sharp pain travels across my shoulder blades. It pauses and then radiates toward the back of my neck. It dulls as it moves, and then gets sharp again. I have never had pain in my upper back like this before. What did I do to cause this? Was I lifting something heavy or leaning over something for a long time? Not that I can remember. But have I ever sat cross-legged on the floor with no back support as I am now? I doubt it. Maybe everybody feels this kind of pain the first time they meditate.

You must stop focusing on it, a thought in the teacher's voice says. *It will make it more unbearable. You should be watching your breath.*

But not much happens when I do that, except a pain in the nose, I reply, but do it anyway. Air seems to be going in my left nostril more than my right one. It's like twisting a towel. My left nose-hole tightens with each inhalation. Tighter and tighter and then a moment of pain followed by a moment of relief from pain, which is followed by more tightening and more pain. This is not relaxing. I can't see how anyone can get relaxed this way.

I forgot to notice my breaths for a few moments. When thinking, there is no awareness of the pain of breathing. Unless, of course, I make myself aware of breathing while I'm thinking. As I do that however, I have to keep pulling my attention out of a thought and push it onto the breath. The air goes in, I feel it, my nose burns with it. If this is what the meditation instruction is about, then I am not made for this instruction. The air is breathed in again, and a sharp dot of pain forms in the space beneath my nose. I grab a hold of this dot of pain. I can picture it clearly: a black ugly irritating speck. It keeps changing shape. At one moment, it is round, solid and black like a BB, and then it expands into a hollow clear ball, without a center. The ball dissolves leaving waves of a coarse sensation like that of rubbing one's fingers on sandpaper. Waves of sandpapered skin sensations gently agitate back and forth in the small area beneath my nose.

My breathing has slowed down. I am less anxious. The waves went as quickly as they came. I wish they would come again.

Now back to the task of meditating. You must try to keep your attention on your breath, the teacher's voice says, this time sounding more like my own. The inhalation at my right nostril, though less in volume, is far less painful. I focus there instead. Perhaps I can improve my breathing through that nostril. That should be good for me, I guess. What is this pain from breathing? I have never had it before. Is there something wrong with me? Could I have a sinus infection? Or some kind of respiratory ailment?

That could be. I should get it checked after the retreat. But now, I should bring my attention back to my breath. It is faster now. My thoughts just then made me anxious. I wonder if any of the people around me can hear me breathing. I can hear some of them, so why wouldn't they hear me?

The man on my right breathes slow and steady, and on the exhale, I hear a muted sigh. The woman across the aisle on my left, who must be a college student, seemingly athletic in her yoga pants and tight low-cut top, breathes more rapidly and unevenly. Every few breaths she takes a long, intentional inhale, holds it for a long time, and then exhales. Then she lets her breathing slip back to a less forced rhythm, that is uneven, but not as loud. My breathing isn't nearly as noisy as those 2 people's, but it certainly isn't quiet and calming.

I should not have thought about the woman next to me. There is something thrilling about her. My heart beats faster and I become nervous and self-conscious. I imagine speaking to her. Then I imagine her being interested in me. This is starting to go too far. I bring my attention back to my right nostril and this time try to feel the touch of air crossing my upper lip. My upper lip seems unable to sense it. But I can detect a tiny brush of air across the outer rim of my nostril after I exhale. It is barely perceptible, so I make more effort to notice it each time.

My inhales are much more forceful than my exhales. I breathe like a machine, keeping the same rhythm, the same intensity. It is not I who is breathing, but my body that is breathing. It is uncomfortable. I want to jump in and change things. That thought causes a change as my next inhalation becomes stronger and the air exits my nose touching my upper lip. If it has to be this strong for me to notice it, then that is what I will have to do. And with that thought, it gets stronger and stronger, more and more uncomfortable.

My left ankle begins to throb with pain. It is scrunched under my right thigh. My foot is also twisted. No wonder my ankle hurts. Why didn't I notice this sooner? It must have been there all the time, and it is only now, when I can feel each in and out-breath that it begins to act up. I must move it. Can I open my eyes? I probably shouldn't. I also probably shouldn't move my ankle. I heard the teacher say that we should not move for the whole hour. But I can't endure this pain for a whole hour!

Fear bursts across my chest: *I will have to endure this pain forever and never be able to escape from it!* This fear doesn't make sense. I could stand up and leave. Then this pain would vanish. But the fear remains: *The teacher and everyone in the meditation hall will see me as a failure*. Shame joins it. Now I am determined to sit with this pain and not make a fool out of myself.

I clench my teeth. Fear leaves low volume echoes in my chest. My ankle pain escalates and tapers off in short cycles, throbbing as though the pain were like a beating heart. No, it is my heartbeat that I am feeling, like a drum pattern behind some loud ambient noise about my ankle. This could be serious! I could be dying here.

Then I check my breathing, for if I am dying, perhaps I have not been breathing. But I am still breathing. The in-breaths are not as forceful as before and the out-breaths are more forceful, being about even. I now feel the touch of the air across my upper lip as a strong sensation that forms a line from just outside my left nostril and down to the lip. The tiny nubs of hair are sensitive there, and it begins to tickle.

A smile breaks across my face and a moment of happiness crests and falls away, very short-lived. My attention leaves my lip and fastens to my ankle. The throbbing begins again, this time with shooting pains every few seconds. My ankle is killing me! I can't sit anymore. This meditating stuff is not doing any good. It just brings more and more pain. I must move. I must open my eyes.

I am looking down at my lap. My legs and body appear so still I cannot imagine that so much pain lives down there. But nonetheless, it's true, as another spasm of pain from my left ankle goes through me. I wince. I look around to see if anyone saw me wince. They are all sitting still, row after row. A couple of people are hunched over as if asleep. That gives me some relief. At least I am not sleeping. But most everyone is slightly hunched over and only 3 people around me have straight backs. I am surprised at how hunched over I was. I thought I was sitting straight.

I grab a hold of my right knee with my right hand and slowly rotate it off of my ankle. Then I slide my ankle out and put my knees together with the soles of my feet on the floor. I won't be able to meditate sitting like this. I can't keep my back straight nor could I hold this posture for any great length of time. What I will have to do is place my left foot on my right thigh while my right foot, which is without pain, will be under my left thigh. I make this maneuver quietly. Then I straighten my back as much as I can and close my eyes.

Back to meditating. It feels like I have been doing this for a long time, that I am now a pro at it, and yet it has only been about 30 minutes. Where is the breath? Ah, yes, there it is crossing my upper lip along that groove beneath my left nostril. And then it goes back in through both nostrils, with the right one being more powerful. In and out the breath goes. No pain in my ankles. None in my back or shoulder blades either. I am a new meditator.

Yes, I can do this. I can become a meditator like the other old pros around me here. I see myself sitting in meditation in my living room while the girls watch TV or play games and my wife bangs about the kitchen making dinner. I sit there oblivious to all the noise. One of my daughters looks up from whatever she is doing, and sees me meditating and she thinks what a special, no, spiritual father she has. Through her eyes I am like the Buddha. Only she does not know I am not enlightened, but I allow her to think of her Daddy that way. My wife then comes in the room and sees her daughter seeing me that way. Suddenly, I am no longer a disappointment to her. She knows that I am a good person, even though I do not help out much at home anymore. But now, instead of sitting in my chair and feeling bitter and exhausted from my day at work, I am meditating, radiating peace and tranquility. It does not matter that I don't lift a finger to help with dinner, or the children's homework, or the yardwork, or the checkbook. I am meditating, pursuing enlightenment for all of us.

Where do I get these ideas from? How long was I lost in this fantasy? It could not have been more than 2 minutes. I must bring my mind back to my breath. There it is! I feel it go in, up my right nostril and down my throat, filling my lungs. My lungs are holding the air in. My rib cage is rigid and tense. Fear returns. I am not afraid of anything as my lungs empty of air, but when the next inhale commences, a prickly fear dances around my chest. But there is nothing that I am afraid of right now. I can't understand why I should feel fear. Is there something I can't see that I am afraid of?

I am always afraid of death, but I wasn't thinking about death just then. I am also afraid of blindness, paralysis, suffocation, heart attack, a tumor, catching a deadly virus to name just a few. The only one of these that apply here is suffocation. The act of breathing, or perhaps my awareness of it, brings up a dread of suffocation.

When I think about fear, I am no longer aware of it. It feels as though I put it in the corner of the room, carefully out of view, while I gaze intently at what is going in front of me. Which is my breathing. Awareness of the in-breath crashes over me. It is a loud bang. The subsequent out-breath is not a loud bang. That is how I have been noticing the 2 phases of breathing all this time: the in-breath is forceful, loud, and dramatic, while the out-breath is gentle, soft, and serene.

What does that mean? I wonder if the teacher could tell me. He must know all about meditation. Probably, it means nothing. I have not had a meaningful experience yet. But it is early in the retreat still. Maybe by the ninth day something incredible will happen. I sure hope so. I don't think I can go on only trying to be aware of each breath without going crazy. I mean bored. People don't go crazy when they meditate. They become more grounded and sane.

I have no idea where these ideas are coming from. It is as though someone is speaking through me, like my brain is a radio. Perhaps I am getting ideas from the people meditating around me. That's an unsettling thought. Their thoughts are mistaken for my own. Which thoughts are mine then?

Bring your attention to your breath! I follow my own command and find the breath somewhere inside my chest. I feel a band of pain radiate from my chest and go around my back to my spinal cord. My shoulder blades begin to ache. My breathing becomes heavy and labored. I am afraid of dying right here and now.

I take in a deep breath and straighten up. The pain goes away. Fear subsides, leaving a trace around my chest. What a relief to get through that! How many minutes do I have left in the sitting? I wish there was a clock in the hall or that I had brought a watch. There is no way to find out. I can probably endure another 5 minutes of this, but no more.

But I don't have to buy that! A new inner voice says, so full of confidence and determination that it cannot be me. And it is very decisive too: if a part of me wants to give up, it does not speak for the whole. I will sit for the full hour. That is it. I must stop whining and start putting my attention on my breath at all times. Only then will I be doing this right. Only then am I in the present moment. That is all I have to do. That's it!

Knower of the Field

The present moment always seems to move in the direction of the future, not the past. The past is the present traversed, enjoyed, manipulated, discarded, forgotten, annihilated, transcended. The future is the present unknown, without limit, empty, unformed, to be transcended. Human consciousness of the present moment is tinged with ideas, emotions, views; mind tampers with it, plays a game with it, and assumes failure and success where there is only emptiness. They are ignorant about knowing/living/being that which is without time. They assume it is like being in the present moment, when in practice, it is more like being suspended in the forward reach and backward stretch of a consciousness that is still and at peace.

Narration

Erik is 26, over 6 feet tall, trim and fit, with thick black hair that is bushy on top and razor cut on the sides. He prides himself on his carefully maintained mustache and goatee, thankful that it takes attention away from his compact nose and colorless lips. His eyes are a deep brown, often consciously projecting a kind of wild energy, as though a genius is behind them. His movements are swift and exact, and when he is seated in meditation, his body is like a solid pillar of marble, an image he uses often to remind himself that an erect posture is at the core of a serious meditation practice.

Erik's Meditation

The meditation hall is just a large living room with a couch and an assortment of chairs that are all taken. Fortunately, there is floor space for my meditation cushion and zafu. Everyone is already seated, comfortably, and I make some noise as I set up my sitting area on the floor. The lights dim as I do this. The bell announcing the beginning of the sitting rings twice before I am ready.

My legs are not quite right. My left ankle is slightly twisted under my right knee as I sit in a half lotus. The zafu under my rear is hard and a little too round, raising my trunk higher than is comfortable. I cannot change my position now. I would make too much noise. I will just have to get used it. Maybe I will just forget about my body after a while. But right now, I feel so unsteady, and my left ankle shoots small bursts of pain.

I will just sit through this. All pain is in my head anyhow. My back is straight sitting like this. That is all that really matters. Pain will come and go. It is impermanent. Now I must begin to meditate. *Bring your awareness to the movements of the abdomen and know each rising and falling,* the stern meditator voice reminds me. I breathe in, my abdomen rises. I breathe out, it falls. I am catching it each time. This sitting is going well.

Suddenly I am irritable. I don't like something. It is a sound. Someone is using a chain saw in the distance. It revs up and roars and then levels off and sputters. How long is this going to last for? I can't get concentrated with such noise!

And there it goes again, revving louder and then sputtering, and then a short period of silence before it begins its cycle all over again. It is maddening. But it is only *hearing, hearing*. I begin to repeat that in my mind, *hearing, hearing,* but soon it changes to *sawing, sawing* and then to *asshole, asshole!* Can't that person see that he is disrupting my meditation sitting! What an inconsiderate thing to be doing! I have half a mind to get up and find him and tell him to stop sawing wood until.... I never want him to saw his wood!

But that is not right. He does have the right to saw wood. Why can't his chainsaw and my meditation sitting co-exist, live in harmony? It is my anger that makes it impossible. What if I just note *anger, anger*? Will that take away my anger and make the chain saw bearable?

I say *anger, anger* to myself, but whenever I hear the chainsaw, anger renews itself, with more energy. I try noting *hearing, hearing* for a while and then *anger, anger* and then *planning, planning* as my mind conjures up a scenario of my going over to the man cutting wood and yelling at him to turn his chainsaw off.

What is happening to me? *Noting* is not working. Maybe I should try *metta*, loving-kindness meditation. I now wish happiness and freedom from suffering for the man with the chainsaw. I say, *May he be happy,* saying it a few times in my mind, but then I resent this person—why should he be happy while I am miserable? Then I say, *May I be free from suffering,* which rings true to my present yearning for peace and quiet. And I begin to feel less enraged, so it is working, though I feel hurt, offended, disrespected. My suffering is due to someone else's lack of consideration. Others make me mad. They do things that set off my anger.

When I emerge from that train of thought the chainsaw noise is gone. The room is quiet. I cannot even hear the breathing of others. My lower back has a dull ache and I am sitting hunched over. My left ankle does not hurt, but my whole left calf has fallen asleep. All this was going on when I was occupied with the sawing noise. I had no idea during that time that I had forgotten my body. I will just have to go through the pain of my leg waking up. It is impermanent.

As I repeat *it is impermanent,* I project my awareness along my left leg, sending a wakeup call to my sleeping leg. Slowly the numbness in my leg begins to evaporate and I wiggle my left ankle to hasten the wakening process. A sharp pain shoots through my leg and I grit my teeth. Another few bursts of pain and then the numbness disappears completely and my leg is as it should be. Now for my back. I straighten up, gritting my teeth for a moment. Then I relax my jaw and make minute adjustments in my back posture so I require less energy to keep my back straight. It reaches a nice balance and then I rest for a moment, basking in the satisfaction of achieving an upright posture. Now I can bring my attention to the rise and fall of my abdomen and begin meditating again.

My abdomen collapses, tightening in, and I note *falling, falling.* It bulges, stretching out, and I note *rising, rising.* Between each rising and falling, falling and rising, I try to notice my skin tightening and stretching, but there are occasional moments of no sensation.

This is going well. My breathing is uniform. My mind does not stray. My body no longer distracts me with its aches. I am hunched over however, and whenever I straighten up, I soon start tipping forward and end up hunched over again. But my attention has not wavered from my abdomen for a good 5 minutes. I am doing it right now. I am alert, awake, present.

My mind forms an image of someone blowing into a brown paper bag. The crisp brown paper expands to almost bursting and then contracts into a shrunken form. It is blown with force and it is deflated with force. It inflates and deflates quickly, like some kind of pump, and then it bursts open. An immense brilliant white light engulfs me. An inner warmth wells up. Suspended in soothing heat, calm radiates down to my toes and fingertips.

My attention returns to the abdomen. I feel refreshed and radiantly calmed. But I must abandon that pleasure and keep my attention fixed on the abdomen. Only by maintaining awareness of the rise and fall of my abdomen will I arrive at *Nibbana*. To do that, I must not cling to any experiences.

I put my attention back on the abdomen. My mind feels cleansed of all distractions. I am neither bored nor restless. This should be easy. I remain glued to the rise and fall. That is the last thing I remember before hearing the soft resonance of the brass bowl ringing, announcing the end of the meditation sitting. It sounded to me as though I were underwater and the bell lay just above the surface.

I open my eyes slowly. What before seemed dark now hurts my eyes. I am all hunched over, and my rear slipped off of my zafu. I must have dozed off—another meditation sitting where I fell asleep. When will I ever become always mindful?

Knower of the Field

Nothing arises from emptiness, not even consciousness. Consciousness folds back into emptiness, and when it returns, the impression of it arising from emptiness is created. Emptiness is not just a substratum of consciousness, or its shadowy twin, but its connection with the uncreated, the unborn, Nibbana.

Just as the body has the five external senses, consciousness has the mind realm, a world that is full of ideas, memories, impressions, performed and contemplated actions, habits and predilections. In that realm, everything arises in tandem, molded into clusters that give the appearance of being whole and solid. Between the parts of these clusters, and surrounding the whole, is emptiness. When consciousness knows a cluster, and touches the emptiness that is of it, consciousness falls back into emptiness.

It does not arise from it. On the contrary, without the arising of consciousness, there is no such thing as emptiness.

Narration

Penelope is making dinner. She and Erik have invited Kevin to join them for a meal and a meditation sitting afterwards. It has been 3 months since Kevin's 10-day retreat, 2 months since Erik's last retreat, and over a year since Penelope last meditated at a retreat longer than a single day.

She has been feeling some guilt lately about how long it has been since her last retreat. On top of that, she often forgets to sit every day, and when she does, she imagines she is starting over, dreading the onset of pain, restlessness, and discomfort. About half-way through, she usually begins hoping for her sittings to end soon. She does not talk about this openly with Erik. He has no problem sitting for an hour every day and would not be overly sympathetic to her lazy attitude. In his presence, she says as little as possible about her meditation sittings, often just stating how many minutes long her sittings are and that she feels better afterwards. Tonight, with Kevin coming over for dinner, she may be forced to say more about her meditation practice; so, as she throws together a tabbouleh salad, she prepares a story of her meditation sittings over the last 3 months that puts her practice into a serious light.

Kevin has never been to Erik and Penelope's house before. It is not hard to find. The address is painted on the curb and her car is in the driveway. The house is smaller than his, perhaps a two-bedroom, and much older, built in the fifties, without much of a foundation and thin wooden walls. He rings the doorbell. Penelope comes to the door. She is wearing jeans and a blue cotton blouse, looking very casual. Kevin is dressed in his work clothes, slacks and a dress shirt, minus the tie. He is holding a long metal baking pan in his hands, covered with tin foil. Penelope asks him what is in the pan before leading him into the house.

"It's eggplant parmesan," he says as she leads him through the small living room and into the kitchen, which is about as large as the living room, with a round table for four at the far end.

Erik enters through the hallway. He is wearing sweat pants and a T-shirt. He comes over to Kevin and introduces himself, offering his right hand. They shake hands. Penelope asks if they would like something to drink. "Sure," they say. Erik goes over and gets himself a glass of water from the filtered water dispenser and asks Kevin if he would like some. "Sure," Kevin says, a bit nervously.

They sit down and sip their water. Kevin asks Erik the age of the house, which he ignores. Erik wants to talk about meditation, for he has no one except Penelope to talk to and she has been distant on the subject for the last few months.

"So, how long have you been meditating for?" Erik asks.

"About 3 months," Kevin replies.

"Who is your teacher?"

Kevin is not sure how to answer that question. He only went to a 10-day retreat and got a series of instructions, but that did not necessarily make the teacher *his teacher*. Maybe Erik just means his question in the sense of *who was the teacher at your first retreat*? Which is how Kevin decides to answer it.

"The teacher was an Indian fellow, from South India, with some kind of long name. He was Buddhist, not Hindu. A former monk, who trained in Bodhgaya under a Burmese teacher. That is all I know about him. I never really talked to him as there were so many people there. One of his assistant teachers, a psychologist, interviewed me about my meditation sittings. His name was Jonathan."

As Erik listens he fills in the blanks, since he has kept up on all the luminaries of the *Vipassana* world. He knows many of them only by what he has heard and read, though he tries to attend a talk, a workshop, or a retreat whenever one of these guiding lights is teaching in town. He remembers having heard about this retreat and wanting to go to it. Unfortunately, it was not at a good time for his work and he had to wait another month to go to a smaller, less publicized retreat by a relatively unknown teacher.

Penelope comes to the table with silverware and napkins. She has been looking forward to this day, having entertained several imagined scenarios of Erik and Kevin meeting for the first time. She hopes they are getting to know each other, and so lingers around the table trying to listen in as she finishes putting down the place settings. She smiles one way at Erik and another at Kevin. She wants everyone to feel at home, to become friends.

"Penelope and I," Erik begins, "started meditating with a Burmese monk, U Sunyata. He came and did a 10-day retreat. There were about 50 people. That was about 3 years ago. Since then, we have sat with different teachers, though all of them part of the *Vipassana* tradition. What I know of *Vimalapañña*, the teacher you sat with, is that he teaches awareness of breathing and then has you become aware of bodily sensations."

Kevin adds, "Yes, that was how it went. We started with awareness of the in and out-breath at the nostrils. On the third day, we began sweeping our attention up and down the body."

"What was that technique like? I have never done it before," Erik asks with enthusiasm, obviously wanting to hear more.

Kevin is now the authority and he feels more comfortable, more accepted than earlier in the conversation. "All of one's thoughts and feelings are manifested as bodily sensations and the mind is able to move them through the body. At first, it's very slow going."

Kevin and Erik both chuckle.

Kevin continues, "But after a while it gets easier and easier to sweep the body from head to toes. Some people at the retreat were able to reach a flow where their bodily sensations all disappeared. That didn't happen to me. Instead, I began to get terrible headaches and sometimes during my sittings my arms and legs would start trembling."

Both Penelope and Erik look at each other aghast over what Kevin is telling them. Erik is about to interrupt with a question, when Kevin resumes, "But the headaches and tremors went away by the eighth day. For the whole day, I felt so light and blissful. I could sit for a whole hour without pain!"

Kevin is obviously proud of that accomplishment, as he well should be, considering what he had to go through to get there. Kevin is now relaxed, having finally told someone else about what happened to him at that retreat. He could not say much to his wife afterwards. She would not have understood, unless she became interested in trying it herself. But that was not going to happen. It soon became apparent to him that she just wanted him to change in a way that made her life more pleasant, and if meditation could do that, then she was all for it. Since the meditation retreat, however, Kevin has been more conscious of his feelings, now that they tend to manifest as bodily sensations and not as ephemeral moods. When something she says and does angers him, he can feel a burning sensation in his skull and the tensing of his whole body. Now he knows that he is irritated by her almost all of the time, whereas before, he would only be irritated in specific situations. But that aside for now, he is pleased that Erik appears to understand and value his meditation-retreat experiences. He likes being seen as a serious meditator, like someone who has been doing it for a while, an old pro.

Erik is so inspired by Kevin's account of his meditation retreat that he must tell Kevin about the last one *he* was on.

Erik says, "The retreat I was on was a strict mindfulness retreat. We did not talk to each other and sat for an hour, then walked for an hour, doing that all day long, taking only short breaks for breakfast and lunch. The teacher was an American who studied in Burma and now teaches all over the world.

The retreat house was small and too cramped for that many people, but with everyone silent, it wasn't so bad."

Kevin nods his head knowingly. "It was like that at the retreat I was on too," he says.

Erik continues, "It was only a 3 day retreat. I wish it could have been longer," he sighs. "I was very sleepy on the first day, arriving toward nightfall, entering the hall just as the first sitting started. By the afternoon of the second day, I was able to note each rising and falling of my abdomen."

Kevin looks at Erik not understanding this reference to the abdomen. Erik picks up on Kevin's confusion and goes on to explain, "There are two methods for observing the breath. One at the nostrils and the other at the abdomen. I prefer the abdomen. With your attention down there, you have fewer thoughts. Try it, you'll see. But anyway, when your mind is on the rise and fall, and there is nothing else—there is such clarity and peace. I had that on the second day, but lost it by the evening. For some reason, I was just thinking and thinking and could not stop. Then on the last day, I was tired and sleepy in the morning and restless all afternoon before leaving. The mind has a mind of its own sometimes."

They both laugh and Penelope joins them, interrupting their conversation as she sets a large salad bowl down on the table. They each take a helping of tabbouleh. Penelope wants them to hold hands and say some kind of blessing, but is not sure what Kevin would make of that, so she sits silently staring at her salad, saying a blessing to herself. Kevin and Erik begin eating without any thought of ceremony.

They eat in silence. Penelope collects the salad bowls and returns with Kevin's eggplant parmesan and her own vegetable rice dish. They each take modest helpings and once again eat in silence. When dinner is over, Erik suggests that they sit in meditation together. Penelope counters with a plea to wash the dishes first, but Erik promises her that he will do them before he goes to bed.

The 3 of them adjourn to the living room. Against one wall, there are a couple of flat black meditation cushions with black round pillows, called zafus, on them. There is a couch facing them. Kevin sits on the carpeting with his back against the couch. Penelope offers to get him a cushion to sit on, but he declines. Penelope and Erik sit side by side on their zafus facing Kevin. Erik gets up and turns off the light and returns to his seat in the dark. He is also the timekeeper. He rings the brass bowl softly twice to begin the sitting.

They are now meditating together.

Penelope's Meditation

May all beings be happy.

May they be free from sorrow.

May they find liberation.

May I be happy.

May I be free from sorrow.

May I find liberation.

May Erik and Kevin be happy.

May they be free from sorrow.

May they find liberation.

May my boys and girls be happy, be free from sorrow, find liberation.

May their victims be happy, be free from sorrow, find liberation.

How is this ever to be possible?

I am sad and happy at the same time. Sad at the horrors of life, happy from the joys of living. Erik and Kevin meeting. I have wanted this for so long. I delight in bringing people of like mind together. I feel for their welfare, desire their success, and relish the thought of eternal friendship.

Should I do *metta* again? It seems to have led to more thought, more feeling, instead of quieting my mind. But I don't want to start *noting*. Maybe I could just watch my breath. It is boring, but not as strenuous as noting. Or I could just do some more *metta*? What should I do for the whole hour?

I think I will try to watch my breath. Before dinner, Erik mentioned being aware at the abdomen as one way and at the nostrils as another. I have always done awareness of the abdomen. I wonder what the breath at the nostrils would be like.

The breath comes in strong, I can smell the eggplant parmesan Kevin's wife made. The ingredients blend together into one smell and I can't isolate any specific scent. I want to smell the oregano and sage, but instead I am more aware of the cheese. That is what breathing at the nose does—it opens up the door of smell. What else is coming through that door? Ah yes, the smell of incense lit before dinner, the perspiration drying in my armpits, Erik's strawberry scented shampoo. The air goes in past a slit in my face hidden by my nose, but before that, a sensation of smell arises. I cannot predict what I will smell when. Anticipation only leads to disappointment, as when I yearn to smell the shampoo and am instead greeted with stale parmesan cheese.

This is interesting in its own way. Breathing is not always what we think it is going to be. I thought it would be boring, but when the sense of smell is added to it, my mind perks up. Can't get too perky however. Trying to sniff one scent alters my breathing, makes it tense, strong, unnatural. And it makes it harder to smell something one wants to. Smell surprises us. Its absence doesn't.

I don't think I am doing this right. I know that I am supposed to note each in-breath and each out-breath precisely when it happens. I've never been able to do that. If I try now, I know I will fail. I just can't do it right.

Terror. I feel terrified at the realization that I can't meditate on the breath, have never, and will never be able to do it. What does it mean when someone can't be aware of the breath? Does it mean that I will never be able to meditate this way? That I will only be able to practice *metta* and nothing else?

I don't want to keep on thinking, I would rather be meditating, but I cannot stop myself from thinking. I worry that Erik will not want to be with me. I can sense his distance. Here he is right next to me and he is in another world. His mind is on his breath and he is becoming clear and his awareness is growing and I am to be left behind. There is no place for me in his world if I cannot meditate, if I cannot go anywhere when I meditate. For our sake, I must discipline my mind and bring it back to the subject of meditation.

Back on the breath, this time at my abdomen. It pushes out and sinks down. Pushing and sinking. Rising and falling. Pushing out like a bloated fish, sinking like a rock tossed into a lake. Fish pushing the rock with its lips through the water. It glistens silver with orange streaks across its fin, pushing that white round rock. Its head turns, the rock drops, and I follow the white orb as it slowly falls floating in the clear water, down, down, never touching bottom, stopping for a brief moment. And then I am back in my body, dazed for a second. My breathing quickens and then adjusts itself as I think about that fish, that rock, and wonder what that dream means, for I must have been dreaming just then.

The fish pushing the rock could symbolize my struggle with meditation. Letting the rock fall could be telling to me let go, to surrender, to drop everything. I have heard that in a

Dharma talk before. On my first retreat perhaps. *Just let go.* That is all I have to do and then meditating will be easy, effortless, worthwhile.

A determination arises to let go of everything that arises. I have a thought of being too undisciplined to do this, and decide to let go of that thought. I bring my attention back to my abdomen and catch it as it rises. I catch it as it falls. It rises and falls without interruption several times. I have no idea how many times. I do not count or keep track of things in meditation. I have a mind-set to only be in the present. In the present I let go of everything, even each rise and fall of my abdomen.

An old memory climbs to the surface. I see my mother leading me to the gate of my old elementary school. I am in kindergarten. I don't want to go through that gate. I keep a tight grip on her hand. She looks down at me. I see that she is worried. I want to comfort her, comfort myself. I lunge towards her bosom as she kneels down to find out why I won't go through that gate to my classroom. I am not hugged. She holds me with both arms outstretched peering into my eyes. I see tears, her face wrinkles up, and I cry too. A wave of sadness, hurt and anger radiate from my chest, fizzing around my neck and the back of my head, an ominous feeling, as if I have been invaded by a malevolent, sad, enraged spirit.

I am crying softly. I hope no one can hear me. No one should be alarmed. There is nothing anyone can do. That time of my life is over and I should just let go of it once and for all. I am not a child anymore. I am my mother's age, 27, too young to be a mother myself.

The crying stops but the sadness hangs in my heart and lungs. I can't believe I am so sad over nothing. It was not a traumatic memory: I was not beaten, abused, tortured, molested, or shut in a closet for hours. My childhood was benign. I was lucky to have loving parents. I was not like the boys and girls who suffer abuse and neglect, the ones I have to help long after the damage has been done, even though we believe we are catching things in time these days. My sadness is their sadness. I have so wanted to hold the young ones in my arms and soothe their painful memories with my loving being. That is not Probation Department policy. We Probation Officers are only there to make sure the kids comply with the courts, stay out of trouble, do their probation in a satisfactory manner.

My life is so empty, so clean compared to theirs. I have no reason to be angry, to be envious, to worry so much. I live a safe existence. I love my life. I must hold on to my relationship with Erik as best I can. I must stick with meditation for our sake.

Yet I cannot just sit and let go of things. I can only stay on the rise and fall of my abdomen for a few seconds. I get entangled in old memories and strange fantasies for long periods of time. When am I ever going to get this right?

All I have to do is pull my mind away from thinking and plant it firmly, unwaveringly, on my abdomen. Once again, I am with the rise and fall. How long will it be this time? I should count each one. Beginning now: 1 rising, 1 falling, 2 rising, 2 falling, 3 rising. I have an itch on my right ear. Should I stop and scratch it? No. I'll stay with the rise and fall. But I lost count. Start over again. Beginning now: 1 falling, 1 rising, 2 falling, 2 rising. 3, 4, 5, 6—I am doing it! Rats! I lost count again.

Maybe it's not the right time to be doing this. I am too agitated, too worked up. I should go back to *metta*.

May all beings be happy.

May they be free from sorrow.

May they find liberation from this world of pain, disappointment, and grief.

May they become free from all attachment.

May they come to know inner peace and certainty.

May God shine his light down on all living beings.

Where did that come from? Buddhists don't believe in God. I have been trying to get my religious upbringing out of my mind these 3 years and here it pops up uninvited to confuse and annoy me. I don't believe in God anymore. God is not necessary for one's liberation. God himself is not liberated. He is deluded. That is what the Buddhist scriptures say. I have heard teachers say that. God imagines himself to be all-powerful, the creator of everything, when he just happened to be born first and everything that followed arose through natural conditions, not out of His Divine Will.

One part of me is angry that a belief in God makes an intrusion into my *Vipassana* practice, while another part is relieved to find a belief that gives a sense of security. I don't have to progress in meditation to be loved by God. I just have to be a good person and develop genuine faith in Him. He asks what I can easily give. So why have I abandoned God?

I have been told that He is not liberated and that those who believe in God will never be liberated. They live in delusion. They do not see things as they truly are. They stop in their spiritual path, satisfied with heavenly rebirth, when they could go further and know the Deathless, eternally peaceful resting place, that which is called *Nibbana*.

But what is it that I want? My immediate response is that I just want Erik, to be happily married, to live a long, healthy, relatively stress-free, purposeful life. That is why I started meditating and that is why I continue.

Perhaps my biggest obstacle to meditating is my uncertainty as to whether I will get all that I want out of my life by doing it. I am asking it to give me what it may not be able to.

I must pull my mind away from thoughts and come back to my abdomen. Or was I practicing *metta*? Or should I just be aware of bodily sensations? Or sounds?

A gentle ringing, pictured as a shiny gold coin spinning on a table top, rises in pitch, and then falls.

The sitting is over.

I have made it through another one.

Narration

From having meditated together that night, they decide to have a sitting group at their house every Tuesday night. Erik contacts some of the people he has met on meditation retreats, Penelope tells her friends, and Kevin mentions it in passing to people he thinks might be interested. On some Tuesday nights, there are as many as 6 people meditating in Penelope and Erik's living room, though most of the time it is just the 3 of them.

They start at 7 p.m., after dinner, and begin with a 45 minute sitting. After the meditation sitting is over, one of them, usually Erik, reads out loud from a book by a famous Meditation Master from Burma. A few weeks later, they get a set of 3 CDs from a well-known American *Theravadin* monk who studied under the same Burmese Master. For 6 consecutive weeks, they then listen to about 30 minutes of the monk's talks, absorbing what they hear without the opportunity to question the teacher. From listening to these talks, they all form the same opinion about their meditation practice: they are lazy, undisciplined, filled with impure thoughts, bound for an unhappy destination in the afterlife if they do not change how they live and abandon their deluded views. The only way for them to turn things around and even hope for a happy rebirth is to meditate with diligence and restrain themselves from acting on impulses stemming from hatred, greed, and delusion. Each week the monk on the CD hammers these ideas into their minds, driving them deeper and deeper, making them seem more and more like their own true thoughts and feelings and not those of another.

They are all affected in much the same way by what they are being told. Each of them feels separated from the *True*

Meditative Path as stated by this monk. There is a gap between how they live their lives and the prescribed *Path to Awakening*. They are told they can enter that *Path* if they meditate frequently, and for long hours. They must also undertake the 5 precepts, take refuge in the *Buddha, Dharma, and Sangha,* and renounce all worldly desires and aspirations. While there is a certain comfort in knowing exactly what they should be doing, that comfort is continually threatened by their failures in practicing the prescribed *Path*. It is primarily because such a clear-cut *Path* has been presented to them that they feel they know, with conviction and certainty, what the *Right Path* is. Thus, in idea, they believe in the *Right Path*, but in practice, they feel so far from ever reaching that *Path* and despair over bridging the gap.

This is what Penelope and Erik are both feeling when they go to hear a different American *Vipassana* teacher speak at a Unitarian Church in a neighboring suburb. This teacher is a man in his early forties who had lived nearly a decade in Nepal, India, and Sri Lanka. He is 5' 8", average weight, and has wild brown hair and a pleasant-looking face. He stands at a podium as he speaks to the gathering of 30 or so people. His voice is deep and tranquil, but not slow and monotonous. He is energetic, engaged, and his presence seems to fill the hall, coaxing the audience to think deeply about what he is saying. He speaks at length about what people experience in meditation, stating that each person's mind is unique and that we still do not understand that uniqueness within the meditative process. The same instructions tend to be given to everyone without considering the way in which each individual's mind works.... The meditative Path is about knowing your own mind—not trying to mold your inner experience to suit a particular concept.... In the process of sitting and being with your thoughts and emotions in meditation, you will naturally cultivate tranquil and beneficial states of consciousness.... If you use force to accomplish inner peace, what is created is inner conflict, not peace.... Too many meditation instructions actually generate aggression, for they are applied with too much force under the guise of being *Right Effort*.... Let gentleness be your *Right Effort*.

That last comment greatly appeals to Penelope. She now has permission to be less forceful in her meditation practice. Gentle is a friendlier way of being. That is what is on her mind when she approaches this teacher after the talk. Before she is aware of it, she is inviting him to come to their sitting group. She is surprised when he enthusiastically accepts and asks her to phone him about possible dates within the next couple of months.

She and Erik go on to discuss plans for this teacher coming to their group. Erik wants it to be a whole day retreat at their house, while Penelope thinks that isn't feasible. She would rather just have the teacher come some Tuesday night. The thought of cleaning the house, preparing lunch, and playing the hostess for a whole day does not appeal to her. In the end, they compromise. They agree to invite this teacher, whose name is Jason, for a half-day bring-your-own-lunch retreat on a Saturday. They will try to get 6 other people to come, making 8 in all, and ask each person to give a donation of $20 to the teacher. That sounds like a good plan. When they contact Jason a few days later, he concurs. They set a date for the following month.

Penelope calls everyone on the phone list for the sitting group. She gets 2 people to commit that way. Erik emails some of the people he has met on retreats, and one of them expresses interest, though he cannot commit until he has had a chance to adjust his schedule, as he usually works on Saturdays.

Penelope tells Kevin at work, and he immediately says that he will come.

As Kevin thinks it over, it occurs to him that perhaps his wife might be interested in attending. That evening, after dinner, he brings it up. She says she would think about it, unless he needs to reserve a space for her now. He says it doesn't look like all that many people will be coming, so she can let him know closer to the time. She appreciates his giving her time to consider it, and replies that she would like to come but would have to figure out some arrangement for the girls. They are not really old enough be left completely without supervision for a whole day, even though their oldest believes she can be totally on her own. Still, she would like to think it over. Kevin smiles and says that sounds good. That is where they leave it.

As the Saturday approaches, one of the people Penelope contacted cancels due to a family situation. The person Erik emailed finds a way to fit it into his schedule. This brings the total number to 6, and if Kevin's wife comes, it would be 7. Penelope calls Jason a few days before the retreat to tell him that they have only 6, possibly 7, people, and would that be enough? He replies that he would come and do this retreat no matter how few people came. The opportunity to assist just a single individual in his meditation practice is enough. This mollifies Penelope's anxiety somewhat. Now the only thing left is to clean the house. When Friday evening comes around, she vacuums the living room, mops the kitchen floor, dusts and straightens, making sure the bathroom is clean and stocked with toilet paper, Kleenex, and fresh towels.

When she goes to bed that night, she knows her house is ready for the retreat. Only, she is anxious about her own readiness as the retreat organizer. *Will everyone like the teacher she has chosen for them?* That is the question that concerns her more than any other.

Knower of the Field

Purified without remaining residue is the perfection of consciousness. Once that consciousness comes to be, I cease to be. When I exist, there is still impurity. When I cease, purity arises.

But I can know a purification, one with a residue of certain subtle taints, which feels like the perfection of consciousness, and is often mistaken for it. The field I know is bounded by the ignorance that is untouched by that purified state. Once that ignorance ends, the boundless wisdom of the Buddha's can arise, and I will cease to be.

Another path is through the awareness of the internal constructed world of my consciousness, where the builder of that world becomes known. When that builder is known in such a way that all future construction ceases, the constructed world within perishes. But I cannot let that happen, even if it may be my evolutionary course. My ceasing to be is akin to the death of the world. If the world perishes, what then will be? I must trust in the perfection of consciousness to go along with this. And that is something I cannot know, so how can I trust in it?

There is no way to just dive into the Unconstructed, to enter Nibbana. It is an endless process of negotiation with the consciousness that is and its faith in the one that has yet to be. On this side, the perfected consciousness is annihilation; on the other side, or so my faith says, the perfected consciousness is the highest, happiest state of inner stillness and peace.

Narration

Jason, the teacher, arrives 15 minutes early. He looks over the living room and decides to place his zafu on the floor near the wall on the street side. On his left is the couch, while Erik's zafu is to his right, with Penelope's wooden sitting bench behind it.

Penelope asks him if he needs anything, such as tea, a cracker, or some water. He says a glass of water will do. She brings him a glass and sets it down on a coaster near his meditation cushion. Sitting on his zafu, he takes 2 sips of water and then arranges his brass bowl, its wooden striker, and his watch, placing them behind him on the right.

Others start arriving. First is Jenny, who is a nurse. She is a large woman, very friendly and outgoing, with blond curly hair, a cute pudgy face, and shiny blue eyes. She asks if she can sit on the couch. Jason says that is fine. Then she drapes her sweater over the couch cushion nearest the teacher.

Next to arrive is Ron. He is the man Erik met on retreat. He is tall and thin, with straight short-cropped gray hair, a mustache, and intense brown eyes. He carries a wide flat meditation cushion, a zabuton, and a small wooden sitting bench. He sets the zabuton down directly in front of Jason and places the sitting bench squarely on top of it. When he is done, Erik introduces him to everyone else.

Then Kevin and his wife arrive. Kevin introduces Pam to Erik and Penelope. Penelope instantly takes a liking to her, expressing how happy she is that they have finally met. Pam reciprocates by saying that she has heard a great deal about her and would like to get to know her. Kevin meanwhile fixes himself a cup of black of tea. He eyes the living room and wonders where he will sit. Maybe he will sit behind the couch, for he wants to sit away from the others. The experience of sitting knee-to-knee with other people on that 10-day retreat left an indelible aversion to sitting close to people in meditation.

Once he has his tea, he goes over to Erik and asks if he could sit behind the couch. Erik hadn't thought of that being a place to sit, though he instantly offers Kevin the option to sit wherever he wants. They share a smile, both being happy to have a good chunk of time to meditate.

Meanwhile, Penelope has gone into the dining room to pull out a straight-backed wooden chair for Pam, placing it in the corner of the room not far from her own sitting bench. Once she is done with the chair, Jason looks up at her and asks if everyone has arrived. "There is one more person, a woman by the name of Joan," she says, and then asks him what she should do. He tells her that they will wait another 5 minutes.

Kevin sees Penelope talking to Jason and decides to go up to him and introduce himself. Jason shakes his hand without getting up. Kevin asks him where he lives, and then how long he has lived there. Jason answers politely, only giving the barest facts. Kevin then stands silently considering what to ask next.

The phone rings. Penelope rushes to get it. It is Joan. Something has come up and she won't be able to make it after all. Then Penelope turns off the ringer on the phone. She announces to the group that Joan can't come. She is disappointed at the turnout. She is upset with Joan, then turns her criticism on herself for not mentioning the retreat to more people. She soon becomes afraid that Jason will not like her and refuse to come here again. She goes over to him and apologizes for the small group. He smiles and tells her she did the best she could.

"Shall we begin?" he says.

Everyone goes to their sitting place and gets comfortable. Their eyes are all on the teacher.

"I would like to say a few things about my approach to meditation. But before I do, I would like to know if anyone here has never meditated before."

He scans the faces in the room, going from Kevin on his left, to Jenny on the couch, then Ron, leaning forward with his legs tucked under his meditation bench, and then to Erik sitting up high on his zafu, to Penelope cross-legged with her rear low on her zafu, and finally to Pam sitting upright in her chair. Her right hand is raised.

Jason asks her if she has done anything like meditation before, such as a relaxation exercise, hypnosis, sitting alone in silence.

She replies, "The only thing I have done is listen to a guided meditation tape. I couldn't do it, so I stopped. That was several years ago."

"What made the guided meditation difficult for you?"

Pam thinks a moment, sincerely trying to remember that experience. She says, "I just couldn't picture things in my mind. I tried to follow the words and do the exercise, but I kept thinking about other things."

Jason smiles and says, "The kind of meditation you will learn today will not be guided meditation. Instead, you will let yourself think about other things if that is what your mind brings up and holds onto. Rather than trying to direct your mind to be a certain way, as what happens in guided meditations, you will allow your mind to be as it is and learn how to become aware of thoughts, feelings, perceptions, and sensations."

Then he turns towards the center of the room and begins speaking to the whole group. All eyes are on him.

"My approach is simple. When you are sitting in meditation, your body is sitting. You do not need to search for your body. It is there, without having to think about it. The easiest way to start becoming aware of your body sitting still is to prefer the touch of your hands on your lap over the movement of your mind. You bring your attention to the external contact of your hands touching each other, or your legs, and prefer that contact. But try not to force your attention on your hands. Instead, allow whatever arises in your mind to be there. Do not push thoughts away and do not pull away from thoughts to return immediately to your body. Allow awareness of your body to co-exist with thoughts, feelings, and sensations.

"Meditating in this way may not seem like meditating should. If you are thinking a great deal, let the thinking go on, and maybe every so often gently guide your attention back to the touch of the hands. If your mind wanders again, let it. Try not to use force. Let your mind lead and your awareness of it follow.

"If you get sleepy, let yourself go towards sleep. After you wake up, just reflect back on the experience and see what sleep was like in meditation. The same is true if you get restless. Let yourself be restless, bored, frustrated. Try not to change it, but just sit with it, tolerate it. Just by being gentle with yourself, your experience of restlessness, boredom, or agitation, your state of mind will change of itself.

"One last thing. If you feel pain in any part of your body, notice that pain for a minute or so, and, if you need to adjust your position, do so, doing it slowly and carefully. If you have an itch, also notice it for a little while, and if you scratch, do so consciously, being aware of the whole process of lifting your hand, touching your skin, and scratching.

"Does anyone have any questions?"

There is silence as Jason patiently waits for any question that might come his way. But none do.

"Then let's sit, with our eyes closed, for 30 minutes."

Everyone, except for Ron, closes his eyes. At first there is some fidgeting. Then some coughing. Then the noise of cars on the street outside gets louder, as does the ticking of the kitchen clock, for all of them are now meditating.

Pam is 30 years old, short and slim, like her husband, though while he is balding she has long thick brown hair. She has dark eyebrows, almond-shaped light brown eyes, and a flat, short nose. Her jaw protrudes a bit, giving her a wide mouth, which houses large, straight teeth.

Pam's Meditation

I skooch back in my chair and get comfy. The chair back is hard against my shoulder blades. My lower back is arched, but that cannot be helped. I hope I am sitting straight enough. Now what did he say I should do? Focus on my hands. They are on my lap, the left one under the right. I can feel them touching each other, but more than that, I can feel my wrists touching my thighs. There is weight, but no pressure. My hands feel suspended. Now what did he say I should do about thoughts? Just accept them. Fine. I can do that.

A truck drives down the street and it is loud, annoying. I wish it would go faster, hurry up through this neighborhood. When it's gone, I can return my focus to my hands, but not until then. The truck stops, no doubt there is a stop sign, and then it speeds up again, but being more distant, it is not loud. Its mechanical growling dies down, but still I can't put my focus on my hands. Not yet. Its growling, grumbling bothers me. It sounds like anger and I don't like anger. I don't like trucks either. Now it's gone. Outside, all is silent. I can now put my focus on my hands.

I cannot feel the touch of my left hand in my lap, and I can just barely feel my right hand resting on my left one. The indentation my wrists make in my thighs is a stronger sensation. I'll stay with that. My shoulder blades itch and my lower back aches. Now what did he say I should do? Observe itches and pains before scratching or moving. How long must I sit with this itch? How can I tell time with my eyes closed? Counting. 1-1000, 2-1000, 3-1000... I will give it 30 seconds longer, starting at 10-1000, 11-1000, 12-1000.... I've waited long enough, why not just move my back a little and have the chair back scratch it?

That feels good, moving my shoulder blades, scratching them with the hard wooden chair back. I hope no one can hear me. I shouldn't be doing this, I know. I should be focusing on my hands.

Now I'm sitting still again, focusing on my hands. They feel hot and dry. I wish I had put on some lotion. Now I can't and I will have to sit for the whole 30 minutes with dry hands. I try to focus on them and they begin to hold my focus. My mind makes up a story about my hands, imagining them to be yellow and dried out, with red sores on my knuckles. One sore in particular rises into view, magnified, and I see all these little canals in the yellow skin flowing into this small red mound that swells and throbs.

What was that? I was gone for a second. I wasn't sleepy. I just blanked out. How strange! I wonder if this has happened to Kevin when he meditates. He tells me you can't really know anything about it until you have done it. I must remember to ask the teacher about this.

Well, at least I feel refreshed. My hands are still one on top of the other, though they feel lighter. The touch of my wrists against my thighs draws my attention more easily than my hands. The contact is sturdy, firm there.

I hear a car go by outside, and then another, and then another, but they don't bother me. My ears turn their engine sounds into buzzing beelike sounds and I begin to feel sleepy. Now if I blank out, I can be sure it is because of sleep. But I don't blank out. My mind forms a bluish haze, like steam rising from a hot bath, and beneath it I see clear blue tinted water, bubbling. One bubble in particular pulls me in, tows me along, and then draws me in closer. The bubble's translucent shell remains solid as I near it. Not the shell, but I, the seer of the bubble, pop, and for the briefest of moments, there is nothing. Then there is floating, followed by softness, calmness, peace, and then drifting into nothing for a long, long time.

I hear a wheezing noise. First the form of my body appears, then the sensation of it. Then knowing an in-breath, hearing the wheezing sound again, knowing it as the breath too. My head is slumped forward. I must have been asleep! What will everyone think of me if they knew? I must straighten up and put my attention back on my hands. A crisp metal hum hangs in the air. Too late!

Narration

As the sound of the metal bell gradually dissipates, people open their eyes. Most of them clasp their hands together worshipfully, while Pam, who has not been on a formal retreat, just leaves her hands in her lap. There is a moment of silence before the teacher speaks.

Jason says, “Take a moment to reflect back on the sitting and see what you can remember about it. Do not force yourself to recall everything. Just see what you can remember without much effort. You can start with the most the prominent events in whatever order they occurred.”

They all begin to ponder their individual sittings. Erik has a serious concentrated expression, while Penelope looks dreamy and somewhat dazed. Kevin puts a hand on his chin as though he is considering or evaluating what went on in his meditation sitting. Pam looks upward with an absent expression on her face. Jenny appears to be straining to figure something out, while Ron looks as though he is still in meditation, his eyes half open, his forehead unwrinkled, and his breathing slow and even.

Jason breaks the silence with some instruction on reporting meditation sittings. He says, “When reporting a meditation sitting, only reveal what is comfortable for you. You can be general about things and you need not give many details. You have as long as you need, so there is no reason to be concerned about taking up too much time. Use your own language. Some people use metaphors, similes, and create their own expressions.

“When someone is reporting, try to listen to what he or she is saying. You may find that you can relate to that person’s experiences and become more aware of your meditation experiences through that. Sometimes, other people can articulate experiences that you may not be able to and thus they can give you a language to discuss those experiences and explore them further. Also, in listening to someone report, you may find that you recall things in your meditation sitting that you may have forgotten.

“So, who would like to begin?”

Jason scans the faces in the room. Only Jenny and Penelope meet his eyes, but their faces are blank, giving away nothing, remaining mute. On his second sweep of the faces in the room his eyes meet Erik's. Behind Erik's bright brown eyes his mind leaps forward, saying something inaudible before his lips move.

"My sitting was filled with *monkey mind,*" Erik begins, looking up towards the ceiling, avoiding Jason's gaze. "It was all over the place. I couldn't get it to settle down. I tried bringing my attention to my breath, but I couldn't stay with it too long before I was off in thought again. Then I recalled what you were saying before the sitting about letting the thinking go on. I became aware how I have been battling my thinking in meditation. So I just decided to surrender."

Penelope and a couple of the others chuckle at this remark. Erik smiles and laughs for a moment before continuing. "I don't know what happened then, but I was drowsy, almost falling asleep for the rest of the sitting."

"Did you fall asleep?" Jason asks.

"No, I don't think so."

"How did the sitting end?"

"I heard the bell. It reverberated in my ear, jarring me back."

"I see," Jason says. "Is there anything else you remember about the sitting?"

"No."

"Do you recall what you were thinking about at the beginning?"

"Mostly work stuff, things I have to get done, and then some things I want to do. I was in the future most of the time."

"And how did you notice these thoughts?"

"I noted *thinking, thinking* and sometimes *planning, planning.*"

"Do you mind if I say a few things about meditation, using your sitting as an example?" Jason asks.

"Go right ahead."

"Erik became aware of how a struggle, a conflict, had been set up between his thoughts and his attempts to be aware of the breath. By constantly pulling his attention from his thoughts and forcing it back on to his breath, instead of creating a state of concentration, inner turmoil was generated. Often noting one's thoughts as *thinking, thinking* creates an aversion to those thoughts and is used to shut the mind up. What changed for him in this sitting was that he surrendered to the thoughts, accepting his mind as it was at that time, which had the effect of making him relaxed. This state of relaxation was not a pure state of calm, being tainted by drowsiness and lethargy. But still it was a more beneficial state of mind than what was going on before it arose, what he called *monkey mind.*

"Now, concepts like *monkey mind* tend to categorize a diverse range of experiences under a single heading, judging them to be scattered, restless, and worthless. Such concepts stop one from looking more deeply into what one is experiencing. *Noting* can do the same thing. If you label all thoughts as *thinking, thinking,* you will not notice the differences in your thoughts and will not be inclined to investigate them."

At this point, Penelope raises her hand anxiously. Jason calls on her.

She asks, "Aren't we supposed to ignore the content of our thoughts and bring our attention back to the breath or the body?"

"That is what many people are taught," he answers, and then goes on to say more.

"The rationale behind those instructions is that if you allow yourself to think during meditation, then you will be encouraging thinking. Coupled with that reasoning is the belief that when one is aware of just the breath or bodily sensations, the mind is pure and aware. In that way of looking at experience, thinking becomes <u>not</u> being aware, <u>not</u> being in the present moment, while being with bare sense experience is considered being aware. But that is only one area of our experience in meditation.

"The way I teach awareness meditation is to establish a foundation in preferring the stillness of the body over the moving here and there of the mind, but that is not meant to stop thinking or create aversion toward thoughts. It is instead a way to have thoughts in meditation and gradually become more aware of them. You are inside the thoughts and know them. There is no pulling away from thoughts, but rather an allowing, a being with your thoughts, and after a while what is driving those thoughts exhausts itself and the mind naturally settles down.

"The content of your thoughts can point to what is driving them. When we are rehashing an argument we had with someone, we may gradually become aware of some residual anger, hurt, or remorse, and it may be one of those emotions that is underneath the thinking, driving it. So, when you are preoccupied with certain trains of thought in your meditation, look for the underlying mood, and once you see it, the course of your meditation sitting will change."

Penelope looks at Jason, having followed all that he said, trying to make sense of it.

Jason stares at Penelope's confused face, and patiently asks her if she would like to talk about her meditation sitting.

She takes a sip of water and swallows it slowly.

"My sitting was much like Erik's. I was all over the place. I was thinking about having people over to my house and if the new people will like it here. I couldn't stop thinking about it. But it wasn't all worry. Sometimes I was very happy thinking about everyone being here and I had fantasies of doing this again and making new friends. Toward the end of the sitting my back began to hurt and I changed position. I felt bad about changing my posture, for I have been told not to do that. That lasted a little while. And right before the bell, I was aware of my breath for a few seconds."

Jason thinks for a moment and then asks her, "Did you allow your thoughts to go on or were you continually trying to bring your attention back to your breath?"

"I allowed my thinking more than usual. When I would try to bring my attention back to the breath, it felt forced. At one point I tried to do *metta*, and that was easier."

"When you did *metta*, practiced loving-kindness meditation, what did you do?"

She says, "I thought of a friend of mine, wishing her to be happy, and then went to a person I tend to avoid at work and wished her to be happy, and then I tried to think of someone who I can't stand and wished him to be happy. It worked fine with my friend in mind, but with the other two people it was difficult."

"You said that you were thinking about people here. Is your friend here?"

"No, she doesn't meditate."

Jason pauses, shifts his attention from Penelope, and speaks to everyone in the room.

"One thing to keep in mind about meditation is that our minds will tend to be drawn to certain things and latch onto them for a while. It is good to know what your mind is holding onto. Not in order to let go of the thoughts, but rather, as a way to know those states of mind more thoroughly. In Penelope's sitting, she was happy at times about everyone being here today. That is a perfectly natural feeling for the person hosting a retreat. From that good feeling, she decided to practice loving-kindness, which was what her mind was drawn to. But she was only able to hold onto it when thinking of her friend who is not here. What she could have done, and can do next time, is practice loving-kindness for the people here, the ones that are foremost on her mind. You can practice loving-kindness for the people it naturally arises for. And if none of them are people you have difficulties with, it does not matter. At the beginning, to know loving-kindness for other beings is a great accomplishment, and over time one is able to cultivate friendliness and compassion for those whom it is difficult to do so.

"Let yourselves be flexible in your meditation sittings. Watch what your minds are drawn to and you will see if the conditions are right to do any of the meditation practices you have a mind to do. Likewise, the best time to be aware of the breath is when your mind is naturally drawn to the breath. The best time to notice sounds is when your attention is going from sound to sound without much thought in between. And so, the best time to practice *metta* is when your mind has good feelings for yourself or another person."

Erik, upon hearing this, interjects, "But *metta* is considered an antidote to hatred and is often taught as a way to eliminate the unwholesome thought and replace it with a wholesome thought. When you are angry at someone, it is taught that you replace that anger with loving-kindness for that person."

"I believe something else is meant here," Jason says. "The *metta* to be applied is acceptance and gentleness to yourself, and in that way anger diminishes. By being friendly toward your own mind consumed by ill-will, friendliness will take seed and eventually supplant the ill-will. To do that, attention must be put back on your own inner experience and not directed outward to the person you are angry at. Only in that way will it truly be an antidote."

Penelope is silent, her expression is puzzled. This teacher is turning all she has heard about meditation upside down. He makes sense in the moment, but will his words really hold up in time? She has never been put into such a quandary by a teacher before. She sorts through her questions, stirred up by these dialogs, trying to choose which one is most pressing. The question, *what should I be doing now in meditation?* looms largest in her mind, but she is not sure if she is ready to ask it just yet. To ask it would take the courage to change from what she has been doing, and she is not sure if that is what she really wants.

Jason looks around the room at everyone and says, "We have time for someone else to report." No one speaks up. He shifts his rear on the cushion so that he faces Pam in the chair in the corner of the room.

Pam smiles. Then she begins to speak.

"I was gone, asleep or somewhere else, for most of the sitting. I can't remember much."

Jason looks at her and asks, "What happened before that? How did the sitting begin and where did it go from there?"

"First, I remember trying to get comfortable. My shoulder blades itched. I could feel my hands in my lap, my wrists on my thighs. I tried to recall what I should be doing and had to remind myself to focus on my hands. At one point, I saw my hands. I mean, in my mind, I saw my hands, but they didn't look like my hands. It was the backside of one hand. It was dried out and yellow and one of my knuckles was red and swollen. Then, for a moment, I blanked out. I wanted to ask you about that. What was that?"

Jason answers, "I'm not sure. I'd need to know more about what happened."

"I just sort of blanked out for a second. It wasn't sleep. When I came to, I thought it was strange. I felt relaxed. Then everything got dreamy and I must have dozed off."

Jason pauses and considers what she has told him, taking a good minute to form what he is going to say.

"Most of the time when we encounter new experiences in meditation we fit them into familiar categories. Before having meditated, or having done something like it, people tend to view consciousness as having 3 specific states: waking, dreaming, deep sleep. Meditative experiences extend the range of consciousness and the new mind states that arise are often initially construed as dreaming or deep sleep, which they aren't.

"This is the area of *samadhi*, which is too big a subject for me to speak about in a few words, so I will talk about it in the talk I will give this afternoon, before the retreat ends. For now, what is important, is that all of you allow these dreamy, sleeplike experiences into your meditation sittings. Let your mind drift, blank out, become soft or slippery with these calm, soothing states of mind, even if it appears you are falling asleep. It is not likely that you are going to fall asleep, and if you do, that is all right. It is good to know what sleep is like in meditation, what it feels like to wake up from sleep with awareness of it.

"Now when you are in a dreamy state and are seeing images, having verbal thoughts, which are usually illogical and fragmented, or are involved in an unfolding scenario, just flow with it. Your head may slump, your body may lean forward, or you may find that you are continually jerking back. Just notice your body and make only slight corrections, if necessary, for your comfort. Otherwise, let your meditative experiences lead without any kind of control or direction. See where the experience takes you. Notice what happens only afterwards. That is, after the first few times of this happening, once you have gotten comfortable with it, reflect back on the experience after your attention returns to your body. You need not go into the details of the experience. You can spend a few seconds recalling the predominant characteristics. For instance, if you saw a picture of something, recall the color and the shape.

"Are there any other questions before we meditate again?"

Of course, there are many questions, but no one wants to ask them just yet. The silent consensus is that it is time for another meditation sitting.

"Well then," Jason says, "let's take a 5-minute break and then sit for 30 minutes."

Narration

Jenny is in her thirties, big and heavy, not very tall but not short either. Her face is puffy with big red cheeks, a small, squat nose, deep-set blue eyes, and a large full mouth. She has long, thick wavy blond hair that tangles easily. She wears a flowing long dress and a beaded necklace, looking like a hippie, though much too young to have been part of that generation. Her movements are well-coordinated and she carries herself with an enthusiastic dignity. There is something wholesome and genuine about her, a kind of innocence, an absence of emotional pain.

Jenny's Meditation

The couch cushion is comfortable. With this pillow wedged in at my lower back it is easy to sit up straight. My bare feet rest on the soft carpeting. They feel cool and I notice a breeze brushing across them. I am just going to let go and experience whatever happens. I like that idea. I like being free to do as I please, go where I will. Like a loose leaf in the wind, my mind is tossed about, staying put for a second or so, and then blown to its next resting stop. There is no destination, only moving.

I love my thoughts, the poetry of them. They bring peace, not conflict. I have always meditated this way. I have tried to meditate by being aware of my breath, but like he said, that creates more inner turmoil. I don't understand why Penelope and Erik always talk about being aware of the breath and noting thoughts away. They don't seem very happy doing that, but they cling to it. I feel sorry for them. They arranged this retreat with a new teacher who is teaching them to drop what they have been taught. It must be hard for them. Embarrassing. While I have clung to nothing all this time, just trying things, like *noting* and *metta*, for a few minutes now and then. But, for the most part, I have just let my mind flow with thoughts, with poetry.

I cannot force the poetic flow of images and ideas. I have to find that particular stream of consciousness, and, as it flows gently on, I place my raft upon its currents, careful not to disrupt its course, and there I am riding along on top of the flow, of the flow, being the flow. I cannot coax my mind, fooling it into becoming a flow when it does not want to flow. No, it will not be as I want it to when I want it to be that way.

There is the planting of my feet in the densely-packed twills of carpeting, tickling between my toes. A wisp of air grazes my left ankle bone and I picture a curl of smoke hanging in the air, coiling. White lines of muscle like smoke that suddenly disperse as if blown by a fan.

Beautiful smoke is what I recall returning my awareness to the soles of my feet. The tendrils of the carpet seem taller, pushing through the cracks between my toes, and I picture them growing higher, green like rye grass in the Spring. In the grass I see a silver S-shaped creature still and lifeless. I am curious as to what it is and so move in closer and see silver scales that brighten, turning into a glistening bright white light. The light glows for a second and then vanishes. My skin tingles. I feel warmth. My heart opens for a moment. I am excited.

White light, white light is what I say, while at the same time I remark on what a great experience that was. I wish I could feel that way all the time. How can I make this happen again?

Then I must find out what I did to make this happen. Was it what I ate? Was it anything I did? Does it have to do with meditating here? Meditating in this group? Meditating at this time of day? Does it have to do with sitting on this couch? Did it just happen by chance? Out of nowhere? Is it from God? Maybe I should ask the teacher these questions. He seems to know more about these kinds of experiences than I do.

What would I say to him? Let's see. I was meditating, letting my mind flow with thoughts when I pictured a silver snake in the grass. I moved in closer and it turned into a brilliant white light. It felt great!

And he replies, *that sounds very interesting. Do you recall anything else?*

Yes. I was aware of my feet touching the carpet, feeling the carpet between my toes. Then there was a picture of tall grass. After that, the snake.

He then says, *you had a samadhi experience.*

What is that? I ask.

It is when your mind goes into a state of consciousness that is dreamy but you are not asleep. It is like a waking dream.

How do I make it happen again?

I try to conjure up that image again. I see it again, but not as a picture. It is like a print from an underexposed negative, all dark with poor details, milky whites and mostly black everywhere.

I don't know what to do now. If I can't have that experience again, then I'll just have to go back to waiting for the flow of poetic consciousness to appear.

I put my attention on my whole body. I am still sitting straight. My feet are still firmly planted on the floor. I feel sturdy, awake, but a little unsettled. I want It to happen again. And now I feel my stomach gurgle and become aware of how hungry I am.

Lunch is going to be good. I brought some vegetable barley soup and cheese and crackers. I hope they have a microwave oven. I forgot to ask. What if they don't? I'll just have to eat cheese and crackers. That doesn't sound as good. They better have a microwave.

I really don't want to think about food, about my weight, about my life. I come to meditate to find another reality, a spiritual one that has nothing to do with my body. Feeling my body from the inside like this isn't bad, but I know I am overweight. Here I go again, ragging on myself about my weight. I am so far from the poetry of thoughts now.

I should just give up right now. I got what I wanted from this meditation retreat and I know I can't have it again, at least not while I keep thinking about unpleasant things. Must bring my mind back to the touch of my feet on the carpet again. My feet are not fat and ugly. They are soft and have pleasing contours. I can picture them. They are golden. The toenails are like polished pearls. I peer along the white shell of my toenails, going from the smallest to the largest on my left foot and then from the largest to the smallest on my right foot. It is soothing to go up and down my toes in my mind. They are like a row of white piano keys. I push down gently on one key. There is no sound like I expect. I push down on another key, and, as it goes down, a white light bursts out of it for a second.

There, it has happened again. I don't understand it, but I am happy, elated. This just keeps on happening and I know not how. It doesn't matter. It just is.

A faint but vibrant pulse touches my ears. It is deep and fathomless, drawing me further inward. I say to myself, *the sitting is over, that was the bell.* I try to ignore it. People are stirring next to me.

Narration

Looking around the room at everyone, Jason sees relaxed faces with mostly blank expressions, except from Jenny seated on the couch, beaming a wide smile. He smiles back and gestures an invitation to her to speak about her meditation sitting. No one else notices this exchange, so when Jenny starts speaking it catches them by surprise. Whatever they were to do, whether it be stretch, get a glass of water, or use the bathroom, has to wait until they have done listening.

She says, "I had an experience that I wanted to ask you about. It was a white light experience and it happened twice. I don't know how it happened. I thought that maybe it was God, but I was not thinking about God during any of these experiences. Also, each one was strange, more like an altered state than a transcendent one. I don't know if this is making any sense."

She looks to Jason for some type of confirmation. Instead, he asks her a question.

"Do you remember any of these experiences clearly? Can you describe one for me?"

"Yes. The one I most clearly remember was of a silver snake in tall green grass. And that reminds me. Before I saw the snake, I saw the grass, and the idea for the grass came from my feet touching the carpet. What happened was the silver snake's scales turned into a bright white light. The light lasted for only a moment. I've never felt so exhilarated!"

Her face is flush with exhilaration. She takes furtive glances at the others during the silence that follows. She hopes that the others, Erik and Penelope in particular, now see her as a real meditator. She has wondered about their appraisal of her, since she claimed to be a beginner and was not a student of any recognized teacher. Somehow, that has made her feel less a meditator than the others who have gone on long retreats and could say who their teachers are and talk about what they teach in depth. But now she has a teacher. He is right in front of her, ready to tell her what she hopes will be the answers to her 2 unstated questions: *How do these experiences come about? And, how can I make them happen each time I meditate?*

Jason says, "You were quite aware in the sitting to have noticed this progression. What happened first was that you were focused on the sensation of your bare feet touching the carpet. This took your attention out of your thoughts and brought it fully on to that contact point. Your mind was very agile in forming an internal image from this experience, that of grass. Such images often form on their own and draw us in until we are inside of them, but what our mind needs for this to happen is a particular shape or color. In your sitting, that shape was the curvy shape of a snake and the color was silver. And for a moment you were absorbed on the silver curvy shape. When you returned to awareness of your body or senses, you felt a kind of rapture, with your mind refreshed and clear.

"We do not have any control over these experiences in the beginning. We tend to stumble upon them. All we can really do with them is become more aware of the pattern or sequence of events. The way to meditate so that they continue to happen is to become conscious of the fact that when one of these experiences occurs, it is likely other similar experiences will follow. So, what you do is notice the shape and color of what the mind was absorbed on, if it is visual. When you emerge from such an experience, let the rapture and happiness, if they are present, pervade your body. Then recollect what you saw. After that, just let your mind be as it is, gently preferring the stillness of the body. See if the experience of absorption happens again. If it does, notice it like before. After a few of these experiences in a row, you will have a better sense of the forms and colors your mind is drawn to. Then, when you are on the brink of an absorption, for by that time you will have developed a sensitivity to feeling when your mind is drawing inward, you can recall a previous shape and color and then see what happens. This has to be done very gently, with a light touch."

Jenny is pondering what she is hearing, trying to remember the whole procedure. She wants to clarify something about her experience that contradicts what Jason is saying, but the thoughts are slow to form.

"Some of what I teach about meditation," he continues, "may not be of any use for you today. You may not be able to apply what I say for months. But it is important that you hear it once, so when the proper time arises in a meditation sitting, you will be able to apply this instruction."

Jenny's thinking suddenly comes into focus. She says, "I saw the white light twice, and the second time it occurred when I pushed down on a piano key, which is a different shape, color, and texture than a silvery slithering snake. What seemed to happen is that I went back into what I call, 'a poetic flow of consciousness.' My thoughts changed, became fluid and less rational, and then I saw my toenails in my mind, and that lead to seeing a row of piano keys. The second time seems to be a different procedure than the first one."

Jason is caught off-guard by her description, which does indeed contradict some of what he was saying. He takes a minute to reflect before responding thoughtfully.

"Sometimes our mind goes through the same general sequence, but with different shapes, colors, and textures. We can't predict whether the same images will work again, which is why prescribing a concentration object with a definite shape or color often doesn't work. Or, if it does, it may take a long time for the person to become absorbed on that object. All that I am really suggesting here is to notice the various types of images your mind is drawn to in your meditation sittings and see if there are patterns to the experience that either repeat the absorptions, as in your 'poetic flow of consciousness,' or deepen and intensify the experience of being absorbed. This is a rich area to explore within your meditation practice."

Jason pauses a moment to consider whether he has said enough on this topic, decides he has, and then asks if anyone else would like to talk about meditation sittings.

No one immediately speaks up, so he scans the faces in the room, and imagines he sees a yearning to be seen and heard emanate from Kevin's eyes. So, he calls on Kevin.

Kevin looks directly at him and says, "I was not too sure about your instructions. I have been practicing *Vipassana* and what you were teaching did not sound like that at all."

"What kind of *Vipassana* have you been practicing?" Jason asks.

"Body scanning. Sweeping bodily sensations from the top of my head to my toes."

"That was the technique I was first introduced to," Jason says. "I did that for about 6 months and then I started to see some of the flaws in that way of meditating. Then I practiced *noting* and mindfulness of all movements and intentions. That too had certain inconsistencies, so I had to find my own way. What I teach comes directly from my own meditation experiences and understandings, and has been supported by my study of the teachings of the Buddha as found in the original Pali Discourses. I have listened carefully to the actual experiences of hundreds of meditators, and base many of my comments on that knowledge. It is a form of *Vipassana,* one that is not based on dogma, not derived from theory, and does not involve the taking up of any beliefs, rituals, vows, or authority. It is informed by the awareness of your own meditation sittings, which do not have to conform to any system of interpretation to be understood.

"That reminds me. I plan on reading a section from my translation of the *Satipatthana Sutta*, the Discourse on the Foundations of Mindfulness, from which all forms of *Vipassana* meditation are derived. I believe it supports what I teach.

"I'm sorry, I went on a bit there. Would you like to describe your sittings, Kevin?"

"I've never talked about my meditation experiences in detail," Kevin says, "so I am not sure how to begin."

"You can be as general as you like. Don't worry about what others might think. This is a very difficult thing to do and you are bound to be at a loss for words and forget things."

"All right, here I go," Kevin says, taking a deep breath, exhaling, and then pausing for a few seconds to collect his thoughts.

"In the first sitting I was tense. My forearms and hands felt tight. I wanted to lash out at something or move my arms about wildly. Then my chest felt constrained and my throat got this balled up feeling. My breathing was heavy. I could focus on it. I decided to begin sweeping, bringing my awareness to the top of my head and slowly going down the front of my face, then the sides, and lastly, the back of my head. When I had swept my whole head, I went down to my neck and chest. I got stuck there. There was a tremendous amount of pressure. I felt like screaming. There was no pain, no rage, just pressure bearing down on my chest.

"I brought my attention down to my abdomen and then to my thighs and legs. I felt pain in my legs, but it was more bearable than the pressure in my chest. I continued sweeping down to my toes and across the soles of my feet. There was a kind of heat in my feet that was somehow soothing. I began to drift off. That's all I remember of that sitting."

Kevin looks at Jason for a response. All he receives is a gesture to continue.

"The next sitting was influenced by what you were talking about. The whole idea of letting awareness of the body co-exist with thoughts interested me. I have never looked at my thoughts in meditation. I was taught that I only needed to know my bodily sensations. So, I asked myself, *what have I been thinking about in meditation*? I mean, I know that I have been thinking about all sorts of things in my sittings, but by not paying any attention to them, it appears I had always been thinking of nothing in particular. So, I decided to see what it is I think about."

"And what kinds of thoughts did you have?" Jason asks.

"I was surprised to find that I would think about something for a little while and then move on to something else. My mind would jump from topic to topic. It was usually mundane, like thoughts about what I need to get done, how I am going to approach certain situations at work, what I am going to have for dinner, you know, thoughts like that.

"That lasted for the first half of the sitting. Then I started to have periods where there were gaps between thoughts. For a few seconds, there would be no thinking. I wasn't aware of much else, except for maybe a bodily sensation. I could feel a new thought arise and then I would be off thinking again. But these thoughts were sometimes totally meaningless babble. There was one that I recall. I was talking to someone about basketball hoops, how I don't like the ones without nets. It made no sense whatsoever and was not a conversation I have ever had or intend to have. I had many of these perplexing nonsensical conversations. That is more what they were, rather than thoughts, they were like scenes where I am talking to someone."

Kevin pauses as Jason reflects on what he has heard.

Jason asks, "How did the sitting end? What did the bell sound like?"

"It sounded strange. It was like I was at the bottom of a well and the sound echoed, sounding as if it came a great distance, though it was crisp and loud. I felt great! It was the most relaxing meditation sitting I have had since my last retreat."

"Well," Jason says, "that sounds very good. I was wondering if you felt any of that chest pressure or pain in your arms in the second sitting."

"Yeah, it was there a little, but at a very low level. I wasn't aware of it at all during the second half of the sitting."

"That's good. I'm glad you didn't have to go through that again," Jason says, pausing to smile kindly at Kevin.

"Now, about your thoughts. You bring up a very good point. The practice of sweeping sensations up and down one's body, which is a form of *Vipassana*, is a way to keep the mind busy in meditation and suppress thoughts. Thinking is going on during the body scanning, but you are generally not aware of what the thoughts are—they are just background noise. By stopping the scanning technique and bringing your attention to your thoughts, they once again move into the foreground. You begin to see what they are, while at the same time, and even though you don't mention it, you probably have periods of being aware of your body sitting.

"What then happens goes against what we have been led to believe about meditation. Our minds get calm and concentrated on the thoughts. There starts to be a space between certain thoughts and eventually the logical connections in thinking break down and random thoughts, which are often short scenarios or sentence fragments, begin to arise. At that time you are in a state of *samadhi*, which I will explain in depth after lunch, and may have lost awareness of bodily sensations or sounds. But one is still awake and feels present with the thoughts. Sometimes, there will moments of blanking out, which also may have happened in your sitting. The fragments and scenarios can also feel slippery, sliding out of your grasp once you are aware of them. This is a good development, especially knowing the kind of meditation you have been practicing."

Jason looks around the room, and then down at his watch, noticing that it is almost 12 o'clock.

"We have time for another person to report or for any questions you may have."

Erik raises his hand to shoulder level and Jason calls on him.

"You mentioned *Vipassana* meditation. I have heard the word translated as *Insight* by some and as *Mindfulness* by others. In your view, what does *Vipassana* mean?"

"Well," Jason says, "the word comes from the root *to see*. Some teachers say it means, *seeing things as they truly are*. That definition carries with it a view of there being only one right way of seeing things. I don't agree with that view, so I prefer to translate *Vipassana* as *seeing what has arisen*. Thus, if desire has arisen in oneself, that is what one sees. One just knows the experience of desire, how it feels, what kind of thoughts and intentions form around it, the bodily sensations accompanying it, the relationship one's mind has with it, and from knowing that experience in many of its aspects, one develops knowledge about desire. That knowledge is personal, based on one's own experiences of desire, coming from one's awareness and investigation, and need not conform to any view held by Buddhists. It becomes your knowledge as much as anything can truly be said to be yours. And that is what *Vipassana* is. This will become clearer, I hope, when I read some of my translation later this afternoon.

"But now, it is nearly noon, and I am hungry as I am sure all of you are. So, let's take a half-hour lunch break."

Everybody gets up.

Penelope had made lunch for the teacher and so approaches him to ask him where he would like to eat. He asks if there is a patio outside.

"Yes, in the backyard."

"Good, I will eat out there."

"Please help yourself to the pasta salad in the kitchen."

"Thank you," he says, smiling up into her friendly brown eyes.

Knower of the Field

I am given weight, credence, and that almost makes me substantial, a real entity. Their minds strain to know me, the Knower of the Field, and alas, it is futile, for their minds are on the other side of a two-way mirror. I can see them but they can't see me. They can only trust that I exist; I know they exist.

What is this seeing, this Vipassana, but looking at a reflection of the mind when looking at the mind. There is no real mind in all of this. Just as there is no real knowing without my knowing it.

Direct knowledge is a myth propagated by those whose intellects like to create perfect models. In reality, in my reality at least, all thoughts, feelings and perceptions are known in their reflected form only. Some sensations, however, are known as they arise. There is direct sensing, but I have no part of that. That is the animal part of the mind's range. I am of the not animal, the nearly not human.

To know the Knower is not possible. To become the Knower, that is the trick to all of this talk of seeing, of knowing, of being awakened in the here and now. But, as you now know, I am not awakened. I just appear to be so in the imagination.

Narration

Each person finds a place to sit for lunch. Erik, Penelope, Kevin, and Pam sit inside around the dining room table. Jenny goes back to the couch to eat her soup and crackers, while Ron and Jason sit outside.

Ron is eating a sandwich, slowly and mindfully, taking a large bite and then chewing it for a long time. Jason has a plate of pasta salad and a slice of bread with a few slices of cheese. They eat in silence. The wind blows around the backyard. The air is cool, sweater weather. The sky is blue and cloudless.

As Jason finishes eating, he decides to pause a bit and sit back in the chair. He looks up into the sky, closes his eyes, and exhales a sigh of relief. He is tired. He has given so much of himself, of what he knows, to these 6 people.

Ron notices that Jason has stopped eating.

He remarks, “I wanted to ask you something.”

Jason opens his eyes and prepares to position his chair closer to Ron so that he can hear him better. The metal chair legs scrape along the concrete patio, making a loud grating noise. But both men are not bothered by it.

“I am a Zen meditator,” Ron says, “Have been for quite a few years. At first, I learned counting my breaths. Then I went through *Koan* practice. I didn’t care for that much. Last year, I met a Zen teacher who teaches students to just sit. Are you familiar with that practice?”

“I've heard of it. It is a lot like choice-less awareness.”

“Isn’t that what you are teaching?”

Jason thinks for a moment before responding.

“Not exactly. In choice-less awareness meditation people let their minds go from thing to thing, supposedly not directing anything. It is similar to what I teach in that they let their minds lead and do not try to force their attention onto anything. Where it is different from what I teach is in *allowing thoughts to go on and on* and in *recollecting one's experiences afterward.* Those are major differences."

Ron replies, "When I practice *just sitting* in meditation, I am allowing anything to arise."

"What else are you doing?" Jason asks.

"The way I practice it, which may not be how everyone does it, is to sit with my back straight, cross-legged, with eyes open, not trying to direct or interfere with anything that arises. There is a discipline to it. You have to remain awake and attentive. Your posture should not sag."

"And what do you do if your mind starts to drift?"

"I stop it, of course."

"Isn't that interfering with what arises, namely *drifting*?"

"No. That is keeping yourself awake and upright."

"Well, that's interesting," Jason says, obviously unwilling to go any further in exploring the contradictions of this practice. "Would you care to talk about your sittings during the next reporting?"

"I'll think about it," he says.

"Good," Jason says, smiling at Ron, who smiles back.

"Well, Ron, let's go back in. I think it's time to sit again."

Erik's Meditation

This sitting had better be better than the previous ones. I don't know what is wrong with me today. I can't get focused. My mind is jumpy and restless. It won't stop thinking about all sorts of things. And this teacher says to just let the thinking go on, promising some sort of tranquility at the end of it. Tranquility my ass! I fell asleep in the first sitting and he thought I had surrendered into a tranquil state.

The only conflict I experience in meditation is with this teacher's approach. He criticizes *noting* and does not believe in awareness of breathing. What can be wrong with being aware of the breath? It is as natural, as free of concepts, as being aware of the body sitting. And this whole idea of forcing your attention on the breath. I hardly ever use force. I just pull my attention from my thoughts, like a dog on a leash, and lead it gently back to my breath. There's no harm in that. So, that is what I am going to do.

Where is my breath? Ah, now I feel it at my nostrils. I should try to be aware of it at my abdomen instead. That is the proper way. So, I just bring my attention to my abdomen. It is rising. *Rising, rising,* I say to myself. Now it is falling, *falling, falling.* This is the right way to do it. I don't believe this teacher has really done awareness of breathing and *noting* before. If he had, he would see that... Now I must gently bring my attention back to my abdomen. There it is. It is falling. Now rising. Now falling. I am with it as it naturally occurs.

There is no self that is making it rise and fall. This is true surrender of control, the annihilation of Self.... Now I must bring my attention once again to the rising and falling, but this time it does not want to go there. Instead, my left foot has fallen asleep and now hurts. I can note it as *pain, pain* or I can just bring my attention back to my abdomen. Which will it be? I don't know. It seems that I can't hold my attention on either the abdomen or my leg for any length of time. I am mostly in my thoughts.

Let's start over. Stop thinking and get back to meditating. I pull my attention away from my thoughts and back down to the abdomen. My gut is all tensed now. It barely rises and then snaps back fallen. I'm not breathing evenly. Must change that. Take in a lungful of air. Exhale quietly so no one hears. There, I can feel my abdomen rise and fall now. It is like a machine. There is no-self behind this activity. I am sure of it. That is why people meditate this way: it is clear that there is no-self in the act of breathing in and out. There is also impermanence. Each rising is followed by a falling ad infinitum. Once one rising is gone, that rising is gone for good. That is the meaning of impermanence: gone for good. I wonder what this teacher would say to that. Probably something clever like, *it is not really gone for good if it keeps reappearing.* Which is true in a way. Even though that moment of rising or falling has gone and will never return, my abdomen has not disappeared, my breathing has not stopped for good, my mind has not ceased to exist.

Enough thinking. This must be what teachers have called the hindrance of *doubt*. This new teacher, this Jason, has stirred up this hindrance. Until today I had no doubt about my meditation practice. Now I am all confused. Even when I am doing it right, as I have known it to be, in the back of my mind I question the rightness of what I am doing.

I hate all this thinking. Why can't my mind just shut up and be aware of the rise and fall of the abdomen. Does it have something to do with the underlying feeling in my thoughts? That is a new idea. The best one this teacher has given us all day. What is the underlying mood in my thoughts? He said to look at the content. The content points to it. All I see is doubt, and a little anger at times. Some stubbornness is mixed in here and there. A feeling that something dear to me is being taken away. That's closer to it.

My meditation practice, which I have grown to love, is being threatened. I am reacting to that threat in the only way I know how. Not by being understanding, or by being interested in the process, but by trying to shore up my old beliefs and tear down the new beliefs I am hearing today.

Stay with that feeling of threat. I am afraid that I will lose all that I have gained so far in my meditation practice. I fear that a part of me that was born with my taking up of meditation will be lost. Who will I be then?

I can't say. I can't surrender to a process that erodes a self I have built up, even a temporary one. This is a terrifying prospect. To meditate without the instructions and beliefs I have so cherished and the teachers I have honored is to be left utterly alone and helpless in this vast undertaking.

A wetness forms around my eyes. Sadness floods into my chest. I hunch over in my seat. I carefully move the round cushion under my rear and sit on the flat floor. I am smaller now. I am a sad, shriveled self. I am pitiful.

Sad, sad, sad. It is better than being mad, I say to myself to cheer things up. No smile. No tears too. Just sitting on my cushion, defeated, without hope, alone.

Is this why I meditate?

Let me stay with this and know it more fully.

Penelope's Meditation

It sounds like Erik is changing his position. He never does that in the middle of a meditation sitting. If he can do it, I can too. It is just too painful to sit like this for 40 minutes. My lower back aches, shoulder pain, bursts of it, come and go every couple of minutes, and I am grinding my teeth. What if I just move off of my bench and sit flat on the ground like Erik?

There that is better. If I push back a little, I can lean against the wall. That feels good. I can relax my back now. The pain has gone away.

But I don't know what I am supposed to be doing. There are probably only 10 minutes left in the sitting. Not much time to accomplish anything. That's a strange thought. I have yet to be aware of my breath without thoughts pulling me away.

And with this new teacher, that does not matter. But I'm not sure what does in his style of teaching. He seems to respond positively when people talk about these dreamy, sleepy sittings, which he calls *samadhi*. But I have heard from Erik that *samadhi* is very advanced. One practices it only after having attained knowledge through *Insight Meditation.*

What does all this matter anyhow? The right way to meditate, the wrong way, what *samadhi* really is and what it is not, who is the wisest and most respected teacher and who is not. These are Erik's concerns, not mine. I only want to be happy with my life, and meditation isn't doing it for me. Sometimes, I feel it makes things worse.

If I were to change my life, what would I do? Change my job, break up with Erik, go back to school, travel around the world, learn a language, find a man who loves me unconditionally. I have never entertained that idea since I have been with Erik. I am sure he is the right man for me. I do love him so. I wish he loved me as much as I love him, but he has stayed with me for 3 years. So, that is not what I want to change.

What about my job? I don't fit in at Probation. The other officers look at me funny when I talk to the kids, as if I am some sort of idiot just because I care so much for them. That is why I chose that profession. So I could help children. And I do so little that really helps. My hands are tied most of the time. The rest of the time either the kid or my superiors, or both, make it impossible for me to do what I feel would best help. I feel stuck, trapped. I must seriously consider changing my job.

For a brief moment, I notice only my breath. It is as if once I realized that I needed to change my job, my mind could relax and I could be aware of something other than my thoughts. Maybe that is how this meditation thing really works. You contemplate important issues, the ones that keep much of your thinking alive, until a kind of resolution is reached. And then the thoughts stop for a moment.

There I am aware of an in-breath and an out-breath at my nostrils. The air feels like a feather, tickling a little as it goes out. It fills up my whole body as it goes in. My body remains filled up as it goes out, but I notice my tenseness loosening up a notch. There, I catch the in-breath again, and, my attention hovering around my nostrils, I catch the feather-scrape of the out-breath.

There is the loud clang of the bell being rung. It snags my hearing just as I notice another feather-like tendril of air stroking my right nostril.

So, that was being aware of only the breath and nothing else. I can see why so many people like it.

Narration

"Before I give a talk," Jason says, breaking the silence that followed the after-lunch meditation sitting, "would anyone like to talk about sittings?"

Pam starts speaking from her chair to Jason's right, so he turns around to face her.

She says, "This last sitting went by very fast. Was it really 40 minutes?"

"Yes, it was. Do you recall what happened during it?"

"I was somewhere else for most of it. It was like my mind was suspended in some kind of liquid space, not moving, like a bug caught in amber. All was quiet and still, and when a thought came to me, it would hang about in the liquid mind for a moment and then fall away. At the time I knew what I was thinking about, but soon after I forgot. Then, about halfway through, I began to come out of it and hear the sounds of people breathing, of the cars outside, of people's stomachs digesting food. I thought about how peaceful it is to listen to these sounds. It was better than listening to music. I enjoyed it more, it made my chest and arms tingle. When you rang the bell, the sound was so beautiful I thought I must find a bell just like it."

"That sounds very good," Jason says. "What was the sitting like before lunch?"

"Oh, that was much different. I was thinking about my family. Not my daughters, but my mother and father. They are fine, but they are getting old, and I worry about them. For a while in the sitting, I kept imagining what it would be like after they die. Then I tried to imagine what it must be like after death. I don't believe in Heaven or reincarnation. I really don't know what I believe for I haven't given it much thought. I knew I was afraid of there being nothing, no afterlife, but that fear came and went, and soon I was comfortable with not knowing if there is an afterlife or not. It is funny because I never thought about that before, had no reason to in the past. Now I'm just rambling."

"No, that's fine," Jason interjects, "you were just trying to express your thoughts during meditation. You did it well. It sometimes happens that our mind goes to subjects we would not normally choose to think about. Our mind is freer in meditation. And we don't have control over what our mind latches onto."

Jason turns in his seat on the floor and speaks to the whole group.

"Sometimes, the thoughts we have in meditation lead to a purposeful contemplation of something that when we look deeply at it, we learn a great deal. To disregard such thoughts by trying to return to the breath, or any prescribed subject of meditation, is to lose an opportunity to carry on such a contemplation. As you heard in Pam's reporting, her thinking is not obsessive, it is not problem-solving, it is not fanciful or self-indulgent. It is purposeful. It is about a truth of existence: that we grow old and die. That is the First Noble Truth of the Buddha's Teaching. And the contemplation came to her, first in a personal way regarding her parents and then in a more universal way in the contemplation of an afterlife.

"Some things in her after-lunch sitting will be addressed in my talk on *samadhi*. Before I begin, does anyone have any questions, comments, or sittings to report?"

Ron, sitting directly in front of Jason, raises his hand to speak for the first time.

He asks, "What do you think about meditating with open eyes?"

Jason replies, "The eyes are our most dominant sense organ. When they are open, our attention stays with visual sense impressions. When they are closed, it is easier for our attention to go to less dominant senses, such as touch and hearing. Also, with eyes closed, our mind tends to be more inwardly turned, which leads to a variety of new states of mind."

"But with closed eyes," Ron says, "people tend to fall asleep or lose concentration."

"That is not entirely true, at least not most of the time. With your eyes closed in meditation, concentration takes on a new meaning. The common idea of concentration in meditation is to stare at an object, such as a chickpea or a candle flame. But that is not the kind of concentration that arises in meditation. What happens with eyes closed is that the mind is drawn to an internal image, sound, voice, sensation and is held, suspended briefly, for a moment.

"I am going to go into that during my talk, which I will begin after we take a 10-minute break."

Everyone gets up from their seats. Penelope quickly scuttles into the kitchen to make sure there is hot water for tea. Erik does a few stretches. Jason is the first one in the bathroom, and Kevin walks outside onto the patio. The rest hover around the kitchen counter, rummaging through the assortment of tea bags.

All of them return to the living room before the 10 minutes are up, and some of them decide to take a more comfortable seat. Penelope sits on the couch with Jenny, while Erik leans back against the wall with a cushion behind him and his legs stretched out. Pam moves her chair over to where Penelope was sitting on the floor. Kevin sits on the floor, his back against the side of the couch. Only Ron remains where he was, sitting on his cushion in the center, directly in front of Jason.

Jason waits for everyone to be settled. Then he waits for the first words of his talk.

"*Samadhi* is both a Sanskrit and a Pali word," he begins. "The Sanskrit meaning is found mostly in Hindu practices, while the Pali meaning is used in Buddhism. For the Hindu yogis, *samadhi* is the highest state of consciousness. It is the transcendent experience, union with the One. That is not the meaning of it in Theravada Buddhism, the tradition I belong to, which is based on the Pali Teachings of the Buddha.

"In Theravada, *samadhi* is not a transcendent or mystical experience. It is a natural part of one's meditative experience. *Samadhi* is any state of mind that is free of the 5 hindrances of sense desire, ill-will, laziness/apathy, worry/agitation, and confusion. One way of looking at is that when the mind has temporarily abandoned these 5 hindrances, it has no other place to go than into another state of consciousness, a purer form of consciousness, and that is *samadhi*.

"Now there are 2 kinds of worthwhile *samadhi* in Theravada practice. One is what the Buddha called *samma-samadhi*, *right samadhi*, in the Noble Eightfold Path, and the other comes out of the Buddhist commentarial tradition a thousand years later, and is known as *momentary samadhi*. Since I do not teach *momentary samadhi* and am skeptical of it as being a suitable replacement for *right samadhi*, I will not go into it unless you have questions that relate to it after the talk. What I do teach is what I believe to be *right samadhi*, which the Buddha stated were the 4 *rupajhanas*, the *absorptions on shapes and colors*.

"There is a progression of experiences that occurs once the 5 hindrances have been dropped that leads to the *first jhana*, and that is the area most meditators are working in when their mind becomes tranquil. Let me quote this passage from the *Samaññaphala Sutta*, the Discourse on the Fruits of Recluse-ship: 'When he sees that these 5 hindrances have been abandoned, joy arises. When feeling this joy, rapture arises. When filled with rapture, he experiences his body as tranquil. Tranquil in body, he experiences a purified happiness. Within this happiness, his mind becomes inwardly focused and serene.'

"Thus, according to the Buddha, there are *samadhi* experiences that lead up to the first *jhana*, and these experiences are pleasant. The commentarial tradition has called this phase *upacara samadhi*, or *access concentration,* meaning that it arises solely as the basis for the first *jhana*. It is said that the factors of the first *jhana* are not strong enough during *access samadhi.* Now I will go into what those factors are, what the first *jhana* is.

"The first *jhana* has 5 factors. It has discursive and focused thinking, rapture, happiness, and is born of seclusion. It is a state of consciousness where there is thinking. It is not a state of emptiness. It is has a feeling component to it, one of happiness. There is a bodily experience, one of rapture. And the mind is secluded, which has traditionally been interpreted to mean that the mind is *secluded from the 5 hindrances*. That is true, but I believe the mind is in a state of seclusion, or isolation, when it enters the first *jhana*.

"Now how does all this look in practice? Let's go back to the 5 hindrances. You are sitting in meditation and you find yourself continually thinking about a situation that brings up anger at someone. You try to bring your attention back to your body, or breath, but it keeps going back to that same person, that same anger. Then you may become aware how that anger is really the hindrance of ill-will. It keeps getting in the way, making it hard to stay with anything other than itself. That is the nature of a hindrance. Now you can try some technique, such as counting your breath, reciting a mantra, visualizing a color or picture, and perhaps pull your mind away from being involved in the hindrance of ill-will. But if you do try such a technique, you will most likely find only a moment of peace, and then you will once again be wrapped up in a hindrance.

"What I suggest is that you stay with the hindrance for as long it lasts, knowing it as fully as you can. In that way you will know how the hindrance diminished and how *samadhi* formed. The *samadhi* will be stronger and the hindrance will be less able to dominate your consciousness when the state of *samadhi* vanishes, which it most certainly will at some time.

"Now this s*amadhi* is the *access samadhi,* though I don't like that term and prefer to look at it as the preliminary *samadhi* for the first *jhana*. In it, you may feel drowsy and your mind may begin to drift. You may see pictures, colors, shapes. You may also hear conversations, become lost in scenarios, or attuned to inner sounds, such as hums and ringing. This is the thinking activity that focuses the mind for the first *jhana*. It can be visual thinking, audio, or kinesthetic. As it goes on, you begin to feel calm, pleasant, tranquil, and may even notice some rapturous sensations, though at a very low level. At some point in this process, the mind holds onto a particular image or verbal thought for a brief moment. That moment, of the mind becoming inwardly fixed on something, is the first *jhana*. After that happens, the image or thought vanishes and your awareness returns to the body. Often someone will then feel blissful sensations, of a greater intensity, in parts of the body. The instruction then is to spread those sensations throughout your whole body.

"Several of you have reported meditation experiences similar to what I have just described. Jenny's experience of seeing the snake in the tall grass is a good example. But not all *samadhi* experiences have to conform to what I just described. It is just that this particular progression of *samadhi*, or type of *samadhi*, is easier to detect. There are other experiences which are far subtler and often go unnoticed.

"Usually people wonder about the value of such experiences. Why have them? What do they do for us? They actually do quite a lot. For one thing, being free from the hindrances, even for just a moment, is a liberating, cleansing experience. When the mind is absorbed, as in the first *jhana*, it creates energy, clarity, and a kind of equanimity that one would not normally be able to have. Also, because these are highly pleasurable states of mind, they make us want to continue meditating.

"Some teachers say that people who practice *samadhi* become overly attached to it. They bask in the pleasure and become lazy. That is a risk, but I don't see that happening often. Sittings which have these kind of pleasurable experiences are often followed by more difficult sittings, where the meditator works on developing the faculties of awareness and discernment.

"I have probably said enough, though I could go on. Do you have any questions or comments?"

Each person seems lost in thought. Erik has a question though.

"I have a couple of questions about what you were saying. First of all, isn't *samadhi* concentration? That is the way I have always heard it used."

"The word actually translates from Pali as *mental collectedness* or *unification*. The English word *concentration* was used early on when these texts were first translated, but more recent researchers in the language of Buddhism have leaned toward the idea of *samadhi* referring to a particular state of mind in which all external sense contact is cut off and the mind becomes unified within itself."

"How does that differ from concentration?" Erik asks.

"Concentration, as we use the word, mostly refers to the mind focusing intently on something. We often concentrate so as to remember something or to lodge some kind of fact into our mind. It is a willful, forceful act, and when we do it, we are consciously seeking a particular result. Now mental unification happens when we are tranquil, free of internal hindrances, and are able to hold an image or verbal thought in our awareness for a few seconds or more. For instance, I would not call the experience that Jenny had *concentration* in the traditional sense of the word.

"What was your other question?"

"I have heard about *momentary concentration* and would like to learn more about it."

"Like I said I don't teach it, though I do believe there is something to it, even though the Buddha made no mention of it. *Khanika samadhi* or *momentary concentration* is when the mind is able to go from object to object and still be without the hindrances. One is aware of a sound, for example, then a sensation, then an idea, and then a sound again, going from one to another without any hindrance forming, without any reactions, and without any trains of thought developing. It is believed that the act of noting, and/or the awareness of the rise and fall of the abdomen, will lead directly to *momentary concentration*. The validity of this kind of concentration supports the giving of those instructions. If someone does not teach *momentary concentration,* such as myself, those instructions are of no use. In fact, they get in the way of developing *samma samadhi*.

"Does that help clarify it for you?"

"I begin," Erik says, "to see what the distinctions are between these kinds of *samadhi* and the instructions people use. I will have to look at this more closely in my own practice."

"That is a good idea," Jason says. "Anyone else have any questions about the talk?"

"I do," Kevin says. "When you were talking about rapturous sensations in the body, I recalled how I often experience tingling, especially after scanning my body several times."

"Tingling can come from all sorts of things, but from what you say, you may have had some short *samadhi* experiences."

"I'm not sure," Kevin replies, "since I really wasn't trying to notice anything about my mind at those times. All I would know is the tingling sensation and I would put all of my attention on it, moving it up and down my body. That often made it more intense. I liked those sittings a lot."

"What sometimes happens," Jason says, "is that when we move those rapturous, tingling sensations throughout our body is that we go back into the *samadhi* state. What I suggest is that you allow your attention to leave the body and go to whatever internal image or thought is present."

"I'll try that next time," Kevin says.

"Anyone else with questions?"

Jason looks around the room. Everyone is silent. He becomes aware of how tired he is. It has been a long day. There is only one more sitting and then, perhaps, he will give a short talk to end the day.

It seems like no one is going to ask another question. But just when Jason is about to announce the start of the next sitting, Jenny raises her hand.

"I have a short, easy question," she says.

"What is it?"

"Is there any way to make these experiences happen whenever you like?"

"No, not really," Jason replies. "If the conditions are not right for *samadhi*, it will not arise. That is why many people who practice *samadhi* try to live wholesome lives, for if there is remorse and strong desires dominating consciousness, then the hindrances will be strong. Contrary to what some people believe, diet has very little effect. The only other thing that I can think of offhand to help *samadhi* to come into your sittings is being gentle, kind, accepting, tolerant, and friendly to everyone you meet.

"So, let's take a break for a couple of minutes and then have the final sitting of the day."

Kevin's Meditation

I sit with my attention on my rear touching the cushion. I can feel the hard floor underneath with my legs and knees as well. That is the foundation, what my weight rests on. Coming up from there are waves of sensations coursing through my whole body. I am a still, hard shell within which tingling, throbbing, vibrating sensations flow up and down. I am not the sensations. I do not try to move them from my toes to the top of my head. They move on their own. I no longer try to put their movements into an upward and downward flow, but experience them popping up here, flowing up or down a little way, then vanishing as new sensations emerge elsewhere.

I get a picture of my body. It is a hard crystal statue, like a Buddha statue, still and solid. The sensations are like veins within the rock. I see them now as wavy planes that cut through me at angles. My mind makes a picture of the inside of my body: my heart is a ruby, my lungs are opalescent. I am drawn in by bright specks of blue and orange against a frosty background. There is a sparkling layer of white opal dust. The dust, tingling, spreads through my trunk, arms, and legs, running up my throat and through my face, dancing on the crown of my head.

Back in my real body, solidly seated here in Erik's living room, amidst the breathing sounds and perspiration odors of those around me, I breath and emit odor as they do. This body is not a rock. That was some kind of fantastic image, one that brought rapture with it.

I put my attention on my seat again, acutely aware of how the bones in my ankles press against the cushion and feel the hardness of the floor through the padded carpeting. They are like 2 pins poking at the hard wood floor underneath. I can picture each point and make an ellipse uniting them. In the ellipse I see a frosty white light. It grows outside the lines and washes over me like some sort of creeping fog and soon that is all I see. The white light remains not so bright and in it I see a picture of Pam, framed as though in a locket. She is wearing a blue sweater, her brown hair takes on a copper glow, like some medieval miniature of a saint, and, for a brief moment, I slip inside the picture, too close to see it. All is copper-colored.

Up and down my arms the electricity flows and when it comes to my chest it bursts across my lungs, jump-starting my breath. Quickened, my breathing rides an ecstasy I have never known before. It gallops, and though I pull on the reins, my breathing does not halt, nor slow, but is steady and joyous.

Pam's Meditation

Someone is breathing awfully fast. Is it Kevin? I try to listen more closely, but can only make out the direction and approximate distance, which means it could be either Kevin or Jenny. It sounds like Kevin's breathing though, like how he sounds after exercising. He is so dear to me. I think I now understand what has been going wrong in our relationship.

I have been trying to control him, the girls, our lives, everything. It is that simple. What meditation is teaching me is how to surrender to the unknown flow into the future, to become still in the present moment, to abandon my expectations, question my desires, learn from the thoughts and feelings that arise. I have been too busy trying to make a future that I want, to build the life I think I ought to have. I have ignored the life I have and have not been living it. This desire for things to be other than they are runs so deep, is so automatic, I don't believe I can ever really stop it. But I can stop myself within the flow and be still. That is patience. That is acceptance. That is loving-kindness.

I am still so new at this that I really don't know what all these words mean. My mind is just rambling, though the thoughts sound good. How can I tell whether this is a useful contemplation or not? Who do I ask? Am I really qualified to be the judge? That is probably why some meditation teachers teach people to take their attention off of thoughts and put it back on the body. They don't want to have to sort through what is meaningful and what is meaningless in their students' thinking. Is this thinking, right now, meaningful? I can't say. And if I can't say that, then why bother thinking at all. But I have no choice in the matter, for thoughts come to me. But I can choose what thoughts to pursue, to a degree, can't I?

No, I really can't. I will be thinking till I die and I won't really have a choice about what thoughts I entertain. Even my future thoughts, my controlling thoughts, come upon me without my choosing them, and I make them mine. Worse than that, I act on them automatically, without thinking.

I have heard Kevin say that existence is a burning house. That picture fits what I am thinking about. I am the fiery thoughts that consume my life. There is no reasoning with fire, there is no behavior modification, it just does what it does regardless. It needs fuel however. What is the fuel of thoughts? If I knew that, perhaps this life would not be a burning house.

I can't wait to get home to my girls. I can't wait for this sitting to end. I am impatient now.

I now know too much. I know that the pain I have always tried to remove is here to stay for good. I do not know how to remove it. Meditating, right now, is just not doing it.

I would like to lie down on the floor. I was very calm and dreamy before I heard Kevin's breathing, which triggered a whole onslaught of thoughts. Maybe if I laid down, I could get back to that peaceful state. That is what I want out of meditation. Though, who knows, maybe my contemplations *are* profitable.

Anyhow, I must open my eyes to see where there is enough floor space to lie down, and then get up from the chair quietly and stretch out on the carpeting.

Jenny's Meditation

Someone is coming my way. With my eyes closed, that is scary, like encountering some unknown intruder in your living room at night. I must open my eyes. It is Pam. She is walking over to the other side of the couch, passing in front of Kevin. I can't see her sit, but I can hear her stretching out to lie down on the floor. Why do that when there could only be a few minutes left in the sitting? Perhaps she had had enough and just couldn't sit anymore. I don't blame her. This has been a lot of sitting, a lot more than I had bargained for.

It has been good though. I have never felt this calm several sittings in row. This is easy. It suits me. I wonder if Jason is having a retreat I can go to in the near future. I would like to continue meditating like this and I like his instruction. He has a good way of listening to people and responding to them. I feel like I am in competent hands.

Should I just allow myself to think and think until the bell rings? Is there any harm in it? What would Jason say? He would probably talk about underlying moods, something that is driving the thinking. I wonder about that. What would be driving my thoughts right now? Wanting the sitting to end, wanting to move about, wanting to be somewhere else, wanting to feel those pleasurable states of mind again, a whole array of wants. But I don't quite feel desire as strongly as I feel restlessness. Because I am restless right now, my thoughts produce wants. Where is that restlessness located? I feel it as thought, not as bodily sensation, so the only location is in my head. What about my heart? Could it be there. A restless heart. That sounds right.

Putting my attention on my heart area, I feel some faint vibrations. It is not restlessness. It is anxiety. I am anxious underneath all this. Anxiousness supporting restlessness producing thoughts of desire, that is the chain. But anxiousness has to be supported by something else. What is lying below it, propping it up? The vibrations in my chest turn cold and I catch the icy touch of fear. Fear underlies this anxiousness. But what underlies fear?

I wait in the darkness of my inner world, holding a flicker of fear in my chest. It dies for a moment, and then revives itself, as I patiently wait to see what supports it, what seems to feed it. My mind becomes incredibly still. No thought for a moment, just a tiny spark of fear, which is then blown out. I return to consciousness knowing no fear for a second but not remembering anything about where I was.

What supports fear? Or is fear the end of the chain, from where all desire, restlessness, and worry come? I cannot probe any deeper than my mind is able to.

The bell sounds dimmed this time. The end of the sitting has arrived. Now I wish I had more time.

Narration

"Would anyone like to talk about sittings, or have any questions, before we end?" Jason asks.

Jenny has a question.

"Do you have any retreats planned for the near future?"

"Yes. I have one next weekend as a matter of fact. It is at a retreat house in the mountains. You are welcome to come."

"What about next month?"

"I don't have anything planned. But if you give me your name and address, I will keep you informed about my retreats and workshops."

Penelope then offers to make a list with everyone's information for Jason.

"Is there anything else? I know I have covered a lot of ground today, but if you have any questions for me before I go, that is fine."

There is silence. It lasts for over a minute. Jason looks down at his watch. There are still 20 minutes left.

"If there are no questions, then I would like to end today's workshop by reading a translation I have been working on. It is of the *Satipatthana Sutta*, from which all forms of *Vipassana* Meditation are derived. I will read the last section, which I have abridged. It is on the awareness of mental phenomena."

People get comfortable as Jason pulls out a manuscript from a large envelope. He flips through it until he finds the right page. He takes a sip of water and begins reading.

Bhikkhus!
How does
a person
meditate
as one who looks deeply into
fundamental truths within mental processes?
Here,
he meditates
on the five-walled cage
that imprisons him in samsara.
How does
a person
meditate
to remove the walls of this cage?
He knows,
"I am seeking out sensual pleasures,
or causing harm,
or becoming apathetic and lazy,
active and care-worn,
or doubting
the truth of this teaching."
I know when one of these barriers is present,
that it is present,
and when one of these is absent,
that it is absent.
I know how it is,
that when one of these has not yet arisen,
it will arise again;
and how it is,
when arisen,
it will be abandoned;
and how it is
when completely abandoned,

it will not arise
ever again.

Bhikkhus!
Here,
On another aspect of this practice,
a person
meditates
as one who looks deeply into
the fundamental truth within the process
of becoming
and possessing
the five aggregates.
How?
"This is my physical form;
it has an origin
and an end.
This is my ability to feel;
it too has an origin
and an end.
This is my ability to perceive;
it too has an origin
and an end.
This is my way of being;
it too has an origin
and an end.
This is my knower of the field;
it too has an origin
and an end."

Bhikkhus!
How does
a person

meditate
as one who looks deeply into
the fundamental truth of the process
of the six
internal and external realms.
He knows
the organ of sight
and visual objects;
the organ of hearing
and sounds;
the organ of smell
and scents;
the organ of taste
and flavors;
the organ of touch
and sensations;
the organ of mind
and its cognitions.
He knows
that upon both parts of each pair
coming together,
in an instant,
a trap ensnares him.
He knows
this process:
the arising of
the dormant traps,
the abandoning of
the arisen traps,
and the non-arising of
the abandoned traps
ever again.

Bhikkhus!
How does
a person
meditate
as one who looks deeply into
the fundamental truth of
the process
of the seven limbs
of wisdom?
He knows
when he is aware,
now
and in recollection.
He knows
when he is
investigating into the true nature
of his experience.
He knows
when he is
courageous
and applies himself.
He knows
when he is
flooded with purified
feelings of rapture.
He knows
when he is
calmed, comfortable
and at peace inwardly.
He knows
when he is
within a higher state
of consciousness,

his mind unified,
absorbed,
malleable and light.
And he knows
when he is
looking on,
peacefully,
with wisdom guiding
his vision.
He knows,
"When any one of these
limbs of wisdom
is within me,
it leads me onward.
And when all of these
limbs of wisdom
are not within me,
I remain where I am."
He knows
how a dormant
limb of wisdom
comes to arise,
and how
an arisen limb of wisdom
can be made to flourish
thoroughly
and fully.

Bhikkhus,
on another aspect of this practice,
a person
meditates
as one who looks deeply into

the fundamental truth of
the four-fold knowledge
of his noble quest.
What are the four truths
of his noble quest?
He knows,
as a truth
anchored deep within his heart,
"Knowing reveals pain."
He knows
"This pain has its source."
He knows
"This pain has its death."
And
He knows
"This is the path that ends this pain."

The room is silent for a couple of minutes after he finishes reading. Penelope asks him if she can have a copy of this manuscript when it is done, and others also voice their interest in it. Jason smiles and tells them he'll let them know when it's finished. But for the meantime, he hopes that today's workshop has energized and inspired their meditation practice. He offers to return to the group and/or to work with people on their meditation practice individually.

With that said, he bows to everyone while remaining seated and they bow to him. He then puts his watch, brass bowl, and striker away in a shoulder bag. When he is ready to leave he picks up his cushion and makes his way to the door. Erik stops him at the door and hands him an envelope with money in it.

"Thank you for having me," Jason says.

"Thank you for teaching us."

The End